LILI IS CRYING

HÉLÈNE BESSETTE

Lili Is Crying

translated by Kate Briggs
with an afterword by Eimear McBride

A NEW DIRECTIONS PAPERBOOK ORIGINAL

Copyright © 1953 by Hélène Bessette
Copyright © 2025 by Kate Briggs
Afterword copyright © 2025 by Eimear McBride

All rights reserved
Except for brief passages quoted in a newspaper, magazine, radio, television, or website review, no part of this book may be reproduced in any form or by any means, electronic or mechanical, including photocopying and recording, or by any information storage and retrieval system, or be used to train generative artificial intelligence (AI) technologies or develop machine-learning language models, without permission in writing from the Publisher

Published by arrangement with Fitzcarraldo Editions, London

Manufactured in the United States of America
First published as New Directions Paperbook 1638 in 2025

Library of Congress Cataloging-in-Publication Data
Names: Bessette, Hélène author | Briggs, Kate (Teacher) translator | McBride, Eimear author of afterword, colophon, etc.
Title: Lili is crying / Hélène Bessette ; translated by Kate Briggs ; with an afterword by Eimear McBride.
Other titles: Lili pleure. English
Description: New York : New Directions Publishing, 2025. | "A New Directions paperbook."
Identifiers: LCCN 2025010223 | ISBN 9780811239660 paperback | ISBN 9780811239677 ebook
Subjects: LCGFT: Domestic fiction | Novels
Classification: LCC PQ2603.E78 L5513 2025 | DDC 842/.914—dc23/eng/20250324
LC record available at https://lccn.loc.gov/2025010223

2 4 6 8 10 9 7 5 3 1

New Directions Books are published for James Laughlin
by New Directions Publishing Corporation
80 Eighth Avenue, New York

LILI IS CRYING

PART ONE

—Hell damnation, cruelty, lies, deceit, betrayal, tears, severances, assassination, calumny, perfidy, misery and death,
says the shepherd.
He is driving his sheep down the stony footpath that edges the garden beneath the ruined tower set high on the parched, barren hillside, bleached white in the Provençal sun.
—Hell damnation, cruelty, lies, deceit, betrayal, tears, severances, assassination, calumny, perfidy, misery and death.
The mistral is up.
Pale blades of wheat sweep the length of the dusty track. The serried sheep press forward and behind them, the shepherd.
Invisible rain, warm and soft, sinks into the dust.
And the mistral to carry it away.
The open tower a silhouette against the low cloud hanging through it.
A wind swirls. A block of wall crumbles.

—Lili, Lili!
calls the mother Charlotte.
She is wearing a straw hat trimmed with a broad black ribbon.
She is coming in from the garden.
The dark outline of the cypress tree, grown as tall as the heavy cloud of the tower, too close; it lords over us.
She has been cutting red roses in the fat and bumping rain.

—Lili, Lili, where are you Lili? My Lili.
From a window embowered with plants, Lili leans out. She tries to catch her mother's eye.
—Here I am, Maman.
Her aging face, her forty-year-old face, framed by the floral window.
—My Lili, says the mother Charlotte. I was so afraid.
I thought you were outdoors.
It's about to storm.
A lightning flash.
Go in, Lili, go in.
Don't just stand there in the frame of that gussied-up window.
—You were calling for me, Maman?
—That's enough, girly, go inside. I'm coming in now, too.
Crash of thunder. The low gate slammed back against the frenzied mistral, the flower-trimmed window refastened.
And the rain buffeting against the windowpanes, the lowered blinds.
—Lili, bring me a vase for these red roses.
No, Lili, not that one—the other one, on top of the living room cabinet.
No, Lili, not that one—you're not there yet.
That's right. You've found it. Do you know how to put flowers in a vase Lili?
My Lili, I'll leave it to you to arrange these flowers in the vase.
Rumble of thunder.
In the same moment: a lightning flash.
The wind easing.
Rain splashing down
noisily, manically, frantically, ecstatically, qualmed, calmed.
—Don't switch on the lights, Lili! You'll draw the lightning. Don't switch on the lights.
—Yes Maman.
The bowing head of this forty-year-old Lili, her face dark against

the white screen of the windows zebraed with rain, the starched curtains, long and pale.
—Yes Maman.
—Come here, Lili, come closer,
whispers the mother Charlotte. (She is whispering because she is afraid of the storm.)
She is seated in the wicker armchair, its base softened with cushions. With Lili at her feet.
—My daughter, my Lili.
The two of them huddled together.
Thunder, lightning flashes, rumblings, crashings, clappings, distancings, the mistral let loose, the mistral stunned, choked, thwarted, lurking in the corner of banked clouds. The sky disfigured.
Water tromping.
The fig tree in the garden bent double.
—Thank heavens, my Lili, that you and me, you the daughter and me the mother, we love each other in life and can shelter here together in this good and gentle Provençal house.
The calm hour strikes inside the house as, outside, the storm grumbles on.
Why, Lili, you're crying! Why are you crying?
Lili is crying.
And outside the storm has moved off,
the wind abated,
the rain sated,
the fig tree righted.

                                                                   But still, Lili is crying.

—I'm ringing the lunch bell! calls the mother Charlotte.
Come along now, get a move on, come indoors, boarders of my boardinghouse.
I'm ringing the lunch bell! Now is the hour.
It's eggplants-and-tomatoes time, figs-and-pomegranates time, capers-and-peppers time.
I'm ringing, I'm ringing.
The black ribbon around my hat is coming loose.
I'm ringing, I've put on my white lace-up espadrilles.
My ankles are still shapely.
My ringing hand still noble.
Come along now, do come in. Only, please, mind the flower beds.
The gardener handed in his notice—I'm the one tending the carnations.
You're in my home, boarders of my boardinghouse, and: if only they'd say hello, greet me as they shuffle past with their retiree faces, as I stand here ringing the lunch bell.
I know, I know.
I know your stories, my elderly and antiquated boarders, I know all about your spent fortunes, your past glories, your flirtations, and your senior love affairs.
—At your age!
In my beautiful house that I make bloom for you.
Mind! I beg of you, please, have a care.
If you can't pay then you can't come in.
Greetings, greetings!
—Why yes, a lovely time of year.
Old age regreened.
Tenacious old age.

Why yes, beautiful weather, still sky, blue wind, clear air, gentle day. Come in, come in. Come out from under the shade of the great fig tree, come up to the tall door, come in to the cool, darkly paneled dining room, approach the colorful glazed plates, the bowls of fruit, the pewter dishes.

May you each take your share.

No, not two portions all for yourself.

You're not starving.

No need to behave like greedy pigs.

That's the way, be polite. Show some manners. Be generous with your smiles, your little attentions.

As for me, says the mother Charlotte, I have now finally finished ringing this lunch bell.

The ribbon on my hat has come undone. I shall have to retie it in my still garden, under its cool bowers, in the shade of its leafy trees. But here's Lili.

—There you are, Lili! cries the mother Charlotte. Where were you? I was looking for you everywhere.

I had to prepare the hors d'oeuvre all by myself.

Why, what is it my darling? Whatever's the matter?

Tell me all about it! Tell me everything. Daughters tell their mothers everything.

—Yes, Maman, says Lili, turning to face the mother Charlotte, her face the youthful face of a twenty-year-old girl from Arles (the selfsame face that a man once killed himself over).

Her face golden, velvety, soft, soft, very soft, so soft, too soft, and her eyes brown (the selfsame eyes that once caused a man to take his own life).

She turns her waist toward the mother Charlotte, the waist of a young girl from Arles, and her rounded hips under her pleated skirt. She turns her dark wavy hair tucked beneath a brightly colored scarf.

She turns her tears.

The tears of the girl from Arles, who never appears in the story, whom no one can ever remember having seen.

Tears trickle down without spoiling her twenty-year-old face, her round chin, her stung lips, the play of light and shadow on her downy cheeks.

For Lili is crying.

—Bon appétit, says the mother Charlotte.

My fees are high, but they're well looked after. I call out "Bon appétit" whenever I enter the dining room, as the meek hubbub of their voices thins out, falls silent, picks up again.

Everything has to be paid for; I wouldn't give out a "bon appétit" for free.

She pushes Lili into the pantry.

—Lili, my darling, we'll talk about this at nap time.

I can guess the cause of your tears, my Lili.

Dry your eyes, Lili.

As the mother, I guess, and I console.

—We'll speak of it the moment lunch is over, at nap time.

Then they both glance up as Lili pushes at the shut shutter of the narrow pantry window with her hand, opening it onto the sun and the tower, rugged and white.

Bellwethers belling, chimes chiming, sheep sheeping all the way down the steep stony path winding its way all the way down the mountain in the summer heat:

—Engagement, marriage, toasts—love, fortune, kindness and luck, forgiveness, joy, rejoicing, a child—smiles, harmony song and dance, says the shepherd, a slow-moving silhouette against the sun in the sky.

And the bells ringing all around the hill, muffled bells, answering bells, bells jangling all the way down the twisting paths of the parched mountain.

—Dance and song harmony smiles, sun and day, marriage, love, birth and joy.
—Greetings, cousins! the shepherd cries out.
He lifts his felt hat and shakes it—a belated gesture, a distanced gesture as the last, late bell rings out, falls silent.
And the dog.

—Shut the shutters, my girl, and the sun slanting across the faded couch of our intimacy.

Shut the shutters, darling, it is so close, this heat, and I, your elderly mother, shall take off my skirt.

What do you think of my petticoat, Lili?

Now, Lili what is the matter?

She turns over abruptly on the couch reclining in broken sunbeams, lit by the gaps in the shutters.

Come here, haven't you always told your mother everything, haven't I been a good mother to you, my Lili?

As you well know it's our habit to tell each other everything.

You and I. As you well know I tell you everything there is to tell about myself... You and I, we are more than mother and daughter, as you very well know.

Tell me everything there is to tell about yourself, Lili.

Let there be no secrets between us.

No secrets, says the mother Charlotte.

In her petticoat, she stretches out on the sloping couch gilded with dust.

—Why are you crying?

It's nap time, and upstairs, behind closed doors, in sunbeams slanting down from the sky, the boarders of my boardinghouse are resting.

You can speak, no one will hear you.

If you have any secrets, you can say them out loud.

Who'd listen in on us?

They are lying crossways on their beds in shafts of sunlight.

Their old black alpaca wools and their striped twills on my beautiful bed linen.

All my shutters shut.

The garden all around us to enclose our sleep.
And sunbeams darting through the cracks in my shutters, shuttering in the cool of my polished bedrooms.
—I know, Lili, why you're crying.
No need to tell me.
I don't care.
Good for me.
If you please.
Shut up then.
No don't tell me—I beg of you.
There's no need now.
For I've understood.
I've guessed.
Mothers guess.
Didn't you know?
And I am a mother, like any other.
There's never any need for children to tell their mothers anything.
Mothers are extremely intelligent when it comes to their children.
The slow mother-mind grasps quickly.
And so very well.
I understand everything so very extremely well.
I possess the intelligence of your life.
More than I'm able to say.
I have no words for what I see in my daughter's heart.
I read it like an open book—your heart, my girl.
I take a maternal X-ray.
And beneath your ribs your heart, laid bare, beats for me.
Don't turn away.
Don't swallow that sob.
Don't turn away to sigh.
For all is clear to me.
You can look away, but I can still see your face.

Because I am your mother.
Your mother Charlotte.
Naturally, it's about a boy.
It's the story of a boy.
Rightly so.
To be expected.
No, I'll not raise my voice.
I shan't wake the boarders of my boardinghouse by shouting.
We'll deal with our family problems in silence.
But you mark my words, Lili, and at this the mother Charlotte raises her head slightly, using her folded arms as a pillow:
—Lili, you mark my words. You have plenty of time to get married. You're too young.
What more could you need?
You have a garden, a home, shut shutters, where the only dust is from the lit sun, and boarders in a boardinghouse—have you not?
Without you, Lili, what would become of me?
—Ah, says Lili, my little Maman, I know all this.
—Would you leave me, Lili? Me, your mother, who has done so much for you?
Lili, we've never been apart, not once, you and I.
Will you leave me, Lili?
I remember your childhood.
Your ribbons and your Sunday dresses.
I'd tie your hair with a great white taffeta bow.
I bought you a fur coat, you looked beautiful in that coat, Lili.
You looked like a little rich girl.
When they gave out prizes.
You always were prettier and better than the other children.
Your baptism and your first communion.
I managed all that very well.
Didn't I organize a beautiful party for your communion Lili?

Don't you remember? It was a sunny day.
And your school diploma.
I'll say no more, says the mother Charlotte, for I can see it all in my memory: the day of your communion and the day of your diploma.
It was a sunny day
(and I was happy).
Do you remember the presents I gave you at Christmas, Lili?
And you, darling, you would embroider napkins for me.
—Oh, Maman, sighs Lili.
On the faded couch: the mother, cast aside.
Lili in the rocking chair by the fireplace.
—My girl, says the mother Charlotte, come closer.
Lili kneeling near the bed, her head weighted on the flowered fabric, the faded fabric, the furrowed fabric.
They embrace.

—Listen—they're up and about now.
A door slams.
Naturally, they slam my doors.
What do they care if my doors are damaged.
Nap time is over, shutters folded back into place, the sun abundant in the blazing bedrooms.
The sounds of voices.
They're coming.
What do they want from me?
In the garden, my revived carnations.
My doors open wide
and light to make the walls vibrate.
The drafts.
The summons.
—We must get up now, Lili, nap time is over, let's go down.
The cool staircase.
The tiled entryway.
The forged iron gate.
The Venetian lantern.
And outside, the heat spread flat along the garden path.
The bower an oasis in the fire of summer.
—Maman, says Lili, could you give me that money you mentioned?
—Don't be daft, Lili, I'm saving it for the carpet cleaner. Later. What are your plans for this afternoon?
—I do believe, says Lili, that I shall shell some peas.
—Well, as for me, says the mother, I'm off to visit Léa.
She takes her thick straw ribbon-trimmed hat down from its sculpted wooden peg.
See you this evening, Lili.

She heads out into the sunshine of Provence.
Lili watches her go, her eyes moist.

—Lili
Lili!
Low voices in the pink garden.
—Lili!
—Here I am, says Lili.
Her face appears at her bedroom window.
A bit untidy, her makeup smudged.
—There, says Lili, I'm coming.
She adjusts her brightly colored scarf.
She lights up the dark eyes in her golden face.
—There, says Lili.
Like the girl from Arles, she knots the tie around her forgettable waist.
—There.
Hello, hello.
Joyful voices.
—Come on up, says Lili. I'm all by myself.
Voices climb the stairs, and the heat gets stalled on the front step.
—Finally, says Marthe, I've been wanting to see you for ages.
—Me too, says Élise, I've tried to come by these past three days.
—Have a seat, says Lili, sit yourselves down.
In my bedroom.
I'm opening the shutters, says Marthe, there's some shade now. That walnut is a beautiful tree.
—But what are you up to here indoors when you could be out looking for us? Why coop yourself up in your bedroom?
—I'm reading, says Lili.
And what are you reading—is it a beautiful book?
It's very beautiful.
—What's the title?

—*The Prostitute Princess.*
It's very beautiful.
—Well, the title is, certainly, says Marthe. You'll let us borrow it?
I brought us some cakes, look at the icing, two hearts entwined.
Were you born under Virgo, Lili?
Good things for Virgos this month.
So it seems, and she lowers her voice. I came, well, you know all too well why I came. Why are you making that face?
You don't like him anymore!
He comes in every day. You don't like him anymore?
—I'm a Leo, says Élise, paging through a magazine.
—Will you come tonight? He told me to make sure you'd come.
—Maman, says Lili.
What will I tell Maman?
—Your mother should know that you ought to be married.
—Ah! Lili sighs.
—You don't want to turn out like the shepherd, says Marthe. Thirty years old and no marriage on the horizon for him.
Because of his mother.
Also, because he's crazy. You do know he's crazy?
—Naturally, says Lili, I'm not crazy and I'm not a shepherd.
Listen, there he goes, on the path.
—Greetings cousins! calls the shepherd, a little wave.
Empty windows watch him go by, but still he calls out:
—Greetings, cousins! Love sun and joy.
—Naturally, says Lili, that shepherd we can hear out on the path is completely crazy.
—Are either of you keeping up with *The Dream Sonata*? Élise is asking.
—Come on, says Marthe, a love like that—it just doesn't happen in life. So many women long to be loved and they aren't. Happiness is a fickle thing. So you should come tonight, Lili.

—But how can I?
—I have a glut of tomatoes—and some eggplants. I'll fill a basket for you. Tell your mother you're coming to get it. For you, says Marthe. I will prepare a whole evening of red-and-purple-colored bliss.
—Right, says Lili, since red and purple are my best colors, they go so well with my dark hair and my golden skin.
—Let's do our cards, pleads Élise, we don't have your luck and we need to know if he loves us.
All three smile the same smile. Our hearts are always thinking of love, and the need to daydream about it is so great.
—Let's have coffee first, says Lili, this heat is exhausting.
Heads bow over a table spread with portentous images.
Seeking a man.
Bowing, bowing, heads bowing so deeply.
Holding out for a tomorrow, brighter than yesterday.
All three dissatisfied.
Ardent.
Their ardors thwarted.
All three happy.
Their happiness distorted.
All three in love.
Their loves derailed.
I love the King of Clubs.
My love—is this little cardboard man.
My life, it's you.
My shining eyes are for you. My waiting heart is for you.
—You're the one I gaze after, the one I yearn for.
King of Clubs made from paper pulp, you're the one I love.
There is no one else, it's you and only you.
Others come and go but you—you're always here.

*

Evening stretches out in the tender garden.
—See you tonight, Lili, thank you, don't forget about the red and the purple!
The Prostitute Princess, shouts Élise.
Smiles, hands, laughter.

LOVE SCENE

In Marthe's bedroom. She's let them use her room.
For she is a great supporter of love stories.
She is a faithful friend to lovers.
and
How many lovers have been grateful to me.
and
I've seen some scenes
(in all colors).
Today, the love shall be colored red and purple.
So here they are in Marthe's bedroom.
and
you won't be disturbed because I had a bolt put on the door,
you can even lower the blinds.
That way no one will see you crying.
For both of them are crying.
No, not kissing.
Lili is crying.
And the young man is crying with her.
He is a handsome young man.

His father owns a transportation company.
The young man is handsome and he's a great catch.
You love him.

You love him.
And you're crying.
That Lili, Marthe is saying, leaning on her elbow at the hotel bar,
ah that Lili is stupidity personified.

Would you give him up, Élise, would you?
—Ah! says Élise and rolls her eyes to the sky.
Her reply speaks volumes.
More than all the sentences in a book.
(When Marthe has finished reading the whole book in her friend's eyes:)
—You can say that again, says Élise.
The door has been bolted. The blinds are down.
The young man is sitting on the chair between the chest of drawers and the fireplace.
Lili is kneeling beside him.
They're crying together.
He is truly a handsome young man. If he were laughing rather than crying he'd be a very handsome young man.
He's saying:
—You don't love me.
—How dare you speak to me that way? Lili exclaims. Have I not proven my love to you, in so many ways?
Then she trails off because she's realized that she's quoting directly from *The Prostitute Princess*.
The young man is a very handsome young man.
—You know that I lay my fortune at your feet, he says, along with my love and my youth and my life.
—Oh! says Lili. I know, my sweet darling. You've given me everything, and I'm so unhappy.
If you love me, try to understand what I have explained to you.
How could I leave her? I could never leave my mother. It's something that I could never do. For just earlier today, in the gold of this fine weather, we were reminiscing about my communion and the day of my school diploma. The gifts she gave me for Christmas, my big doll, my work basket.
And all that is so very true, says Lili.

True.

—It's not true! shouts the young man.

What's true, shouts the young man, is that you're my woman, what's true is that I love you, you love me, you're beautiful, you're young, and your eyes, your waist, your hair, your brightly colored scarf all belong to me.

And he leans over her. Savagely.

—Ah, says Marthe, leaning on the hotel bar, shrugging her shoulders, if I were loved as she is, I wouldn't make such a fuss. No, I would not make such a fuss.

He leans. Savagely.

They seize hold of each other, uniting, seeking each other, finding each other, attaching themselves to each other, losing each other, finding each other again.

—I did well, says Marthe, to lower the blinds.

—Naturally, says Lili.

—You can't break my life like this, sobs the young man. Everyone has a mother, but we don't all smash up our lives for her sake.

—It's different for me, says Lili.

A knock at the door. Time's up. All gone well? It's Marthe, whispering through the keyhole.

It's tomatoes-and-eggplants time, and I must take them home to my mother.

I added some ripe grapes, says Marthe, and two or three green leaves from the trees over the market. For decoration. In the wicker basket, yellowed by time.

—It's time for us to part.

The young man sighs and turns away.

The women disapprove.

The young man is walking away. The women busy themselves around the tables, their backs turned so they don't have to watch this love that's shattering into pieces say its last forever-goodbye.

He's gone.
Lili remains pressed against the glass door, trying to make out his fading silhouette in the darkness.
Like in the movies.
Then she turns back to the room.
—Come and sit down with us, says Marthe.
If your mother comes looking for you, who cares? We'll tell her we were playing cards.
Huddled together and plotting.
—You're going to do it, says Marthe, and we're going to help you.
You've already lied to her. When a lie makes a person happy, what harm can it do?
If I knew how to be happy, I'd do it instantly.
And for us happiness means love, does it not?
There is no other happiness.
If there is no love in your life, Lili, what kind of life will it be?
—Maybe you are right, says Lili. Perhaps that is true.
—Love! Marthe cries out.

LOVE!

Henri ditched me, but I know where he lives, I'll find him and get him back.

—It's impossible, says Lili.

What she means is that Marthe's unhappiness is impossible.

It's a word of consolation pronounced without conviction and without hope.

It's a thing women say. A saying that means nothing.

Marthe is no fool.

—Hold on to your happiness, she says. Go after your happiness and bring it back.

Me, in my life: I am *for* happiness.

For this kind of happiness.

And if it eludes me, I'll make others all around me.

Red happinesses to crunch on in the sun like the pomegranates I put in your basket.

I need love so badly I'm sick with it.

I want it for myself and I want it for other people.

Don't give me that nonsense about your mother.

She loves you? I believe she does.

But surely we're lovers before we're mothers?

The love you feel for your child is not your *first* love.

What would we women do without a man's love?

I *am* right. What I am saying *is* true.

My life, full of love stories, my love stories and other people's love stories, is the only true life for a woman.

—Ah! says Marthe, if I were you I would not give up on my chance at happiness!

What do you think Élise?

—I agree, says Élise.

I'll walk with you to the bus stop.

—But Maman? says Lili.
Tell her that you're going to visit your aunt.
We'll take care of everything else.
The bus leaves at 7 p.m.
We're your friends, Lili, your good friends.
—Maybe you're right, says Lili.
I'll pack a few things.
I'll take my zip-up bag.
She picks up the basket.
She bids them a last forever-goodbye.
The basket is heavy.
And the colors are dead in the night.

—Weren't you out late, says the mother.
I got tired of waiting at the window. I just this minute came down, but I don't like being out here in the shadowy garden.
—Aren't you cold? It's cooler tonight. Where's your scarf? You must have forgotten it.
You're always gadding about with that Marthe and that Élise.
—We played cards and drank coffee, says Lili.
—Didn't you have the whole afternoon to chat your nonsense?
Let's go up to bed now, and let's switch off the lights as we go.

—It's like this, says Lili.
I left and I came back.
I left and I did an about-face.
I tried and I failed.
I tried but it was no good.
So here I am, back again.
Hello!
With my zip-up bag.
Hello, Maman.
—Here is my daughter, returned to me, says the mother Charlotte.
My lost daughter.
My found daughter.
My daughter who runs away with her zip-up bag.
Here is my deceiving daughter.
My cheating daughter.
Who has no qualms about telling me silly stories
and lies.
—She left me, says the mother Charlotte.
She'd left me.
She was gone.
And what in heaven's name did I do to deserve being abandoned by my own daughter?
Did I merit such punishment?
If only my arms could stretch up to the blue sky and shake those clouds.
For I loved her so much (my daughter).
She has let me down.
I have been disappointed in love. And what a love!
I still love her, naturally, I love her just as much as I ever did.

Only now there's a fresh scent of disappointment to add to the burden of that love.

She was everything to me.

My life, I lived it through her.

I had eyes only for her.

Don't think I pay any attention to the boarders of my boarding-house. I scarcely see them. I always get their old faces mixed up. I'll mistake a mouth for an ear, or a chin, I'll put three ears where there should only be one.

But my daughter's face!

Hers is the face I live with—I have faced it my whole life.

I know the face of my love of a daughter.

I've watched it grow, find its shape, fill in. I've studied every fold of that face.

The thousand faces of my daughter.

But always the same stung lips, the same gold-flecked eyes, the same straight nose, and that wart, though you'd hardly notice it, near the ear. Your dimpled chin.

(I used to pinch it, playfully, when you were a baby.)

I know you like a familiar landscape known forever. A landscape with no secrets, no mystery.

And for two whole days you were gone.

Honestly, it's not the number of days. What matters is the exact moment you left.

That precise moment when leaving seemed possible to you.

I refused offers of remarriage, for her sake.

It's true: I didn't feel like I needed any more love.

What with this one reigning over my life.

—Yes, I'll forgive her. Naturally, I'll forgive her.

Because you came back, I'll forgive you.

Yes, I'll forget. Naturally, I'll forget.

I'll forget my anger, my tears, my entreaties, my bitterness, my lamentations, my hopes, my dashed hopes, the work that I had to do all by myself. (She left me with all the work to do.)
When your aunt called to say that you weren't there.
I'll forget that for a moment my daughter did not love me, that she left me.
Severance.
Forgiveness.
We'll start over again.
As if nothing happened.
Between us all our habitual little sayings.
Our loving little phrases.
—The mayonnaise has taken, Maman.
—Thank you, Lili, get dressed now, don't spend all day in your dressing gown.
—I'm off to the market.
—Are you taking the green bag today?
—The plumber should be here soon.

—Ah, no! That's not how it'll go. Yes, my girl, we shall have ourselves an explanation.
Come to my bedroom and be quick about it, quicker than that if you please.
We'll lock the door.
That way, we shan't be disturbed.
Now is not a good time for anyone to disturb us.
Someone's ringing the doorbell.
No, don't answer it.
Let it ring.
It's not our concern.

What concerns us, my girl.
Bad girl.
Bit of nothing girl.
Bold girl.
Whore.
Streetwalker.
Girl turned out badly.
Girl gone crazy.
Over a boy.
Stupid girl.
And what of your mother?
Your mother Charlotte?
A boy
no one knows a thing about.
Not even his name.
—I know his name, says Lili.
—Well, I don't.
Let the bell ring.
No, don't answer it.
It'll drown out our voices.
We'll say we didn't hear it.
Leave it.
It's not important.
What's important is what's going to happen in this room. Between the two of us.
Your face,
(refound, recognized, returned)
facing mine.
It's well within a mother's rights to slap the face of her twenty-year-old runaway daughter.
This face belongs to me, I know it so well, I can touch it with my hand.

I can slap it. (it's mine)
So I'll know by the skin of my palm that the face I believed was lost (forever, gone, never to be seen again) has come back to me.
Thanks to you, my deserter daughter, I'll learn the pleasures of slapping someone today.
—And what am I to tell the boarders of my boardinghouse! About my runaway daughter?
You're crying! Because of a slap?
Children will always cry over a slap.
Cry then!
Your tears won't stop me.
I'll answer that doorbell now. It's getting on my nerves.
Tell me you won't do it again.
No, you won't do it again?
You promise me?
It's all over and done with?
What's that? You'll not be eating this evening?
You shan't be coming downstairs for dinner?
So once again I'll be setting the table all by myself.
It's not the parents who are tired now, it's the children. Do as you like.
And I'm going to put a sock in that bell.

—It's like this, says Lili. I left and I came back.
I went and I returned.
I tried. But I'm not made for success.
Others might have succeeded. Not me.
I'm not made for glory.
I'm made for defeat.
I'll tell you everything.

Because you're my cousin.

—Naturally, says the shepherd, you can tell me the whole story. I'm thirty years old and there's nothing I can't be told.

And I love my mother.

We've found ourselves a good spot up here, in the warmth of this rusty autumn, in the long shadows of the tired tower.

I've never told anyone.

I've never spoken of it.

Not even to Marthe.

Not even to Élise.

But I'll tell you.

You love your mother and you'll understand.

Your face is like a wall. The crumbling wall of this old, ruined tower. It'll keep my confidences safe.

I can't talk to my mother. She doesn't understand these things.

—Talk to me, says the shepherd, you could even ask the questions *and* give the answers. Don't be embarrassed. I won't make you feel embarrassed.

—I left, says Lili, our plan was to meet Wednesday morning on the Paris train.

I spent the night in a hotel.

I was afraid. I wasn't feeling so good.

I wasn't happy.

—And now—are you happy now? asks the shepherd.

—No, says Lili. Because I'm never happy. Do you know of anyone who's actually happy? Do you?

The shepherd doesn't reply. He's watching over his flock.

That night, she says, I dreamed of Maman.

I may have forgotten my childhood, but that night while I was asleep I dreamed of Maman. I can no longer remember my dream. That morning, I couldn't remember a single thing about it, but it left me with these feelings of anxiety and torment. And Maman lost, deformed, reformed, disappeared, reappeared in the clouds—in repressed, compressed, thinning, regathering clouds of torment. So, rather than taking the road to the station, I turned back. I came home.

I turned away.

I changed direction.

I said: no.

I lost sight of the path to happiness.

I couldn't be happy.

I don't even need to be happy.

When it comes down to it, I am fine with Maman.

I don't need another source of affection.

—Maman, says the shepherd.

—Still, says Lili. I did love him, he was handsome. I'll never love anyone else. I'll never desire anyone as I desired him. But for me the sun has set on happiness.

I came back.

Those fourteen kilometers, I walked them home.

Between 5 and 7 a.m.

In the happy sun of a fresh new day.

I felt no sorrow.

When I was almost at Laudun, I sat down on a bank.

I shed a single tear.

That's all.

I hugged my zip-up bag tightly to my chest.

Now, whenever I see a zipper, I think of that solitary tear.

I'll never forget it.

And I feel my heart pinch.

Just the one tear, sole bearer of so many great disappointments.

—I resumed everyday life with Maman.

Everyday life is good, says the shepherd.

Who needs adventure?

—Is happiness an adventure?
People are saying that I ran away—fled, in a fugue.
—Fugue, says the shepherd.

PART TWO

They are in Marthe's bedroom.
Marthe said:
—I had a bolt put on the door
and
You can lower the blinds.
He is sitting on the chair between the fireplace and the dresser.
She is kneeling.
They are both crying.

Familiar image.
Reproduced.
Fixed tableau.
Love is always the same.
Interminably samey.
Same-ily similar.
Similarly the same.
Likewisely eternal.
We wouldn't change a single thing about it.
Which is why this image shall never change.
They're in Marthe's bedroom.
Cheeks burning.
Fingers interlaced.
Gazing boldly into each other's eyes.
The door bolted.

The blinds down.
Between the dresser and the fireplace.
                For all time.

—Look Lili, says the mother Charlotte, this dress suits me perfectly! It is my own creation.

The fashion is for vertical pleats. I made mine horizontal.

Because I'm not like other people.

Me, says the mother Charlotte, I'll never just follow the crowd.

(I'm naturally better.)

My mother, your grandmother, was a great coquette. An elegant woman.

And I, her daughter, take after her.

We're not like other people.

We're from a good family line, Lili. We're from old stock. You can be proud of your roots, Lili.

Your great-grandfather had an aristocratic surname. He was a "de," Lili.

Which explains why we're not like other people.

He married his maid, that lunatic, and had only one daughter.

But we were a fine family, we were, Lili. When you walk down the street you can hold your head up high.

Besides, just look at all the photographs of your grandmother, isn't she the image of a great lady?

The gold pince-nez, the gold chain of her pince-nez hanging from the curls of her hair.

She had her own way of doing things.

Because she wasn't like other people.

—And neither am I—me, I'm not like other people either.

—You see, says Lili, addressing Marthe and Élise who are looking her up and down, this style of gathering the pleats at the back, it's my own creation, this dress is unique. I wear designer pieces now. My own creations.

This dress is not like other dresses.

And I am not like other people.
For I take after my mother, and she's not like other people either.
We were a fine family, says Lili.
We were from somewhere.
—If you say so, say the women laughing, cackling, babbling, playing, but we know who we're dealing with.
Turn around.
She turns.

—So she did go! says Élise. I would never have thought she'd leave. But she did.
—It's like this, cries Lili, I refuse to go off with the man I do love. Instead, I go off with the man I don't love.
She left, says Marthe, but without saying a word.
She just said something about a couple of days' rest at the seaside.
—That's what she told us.
—That's what she told her mother.
And her mother who had her sewing some summer dresses, because that's where she thought she was going. A whole trousseau.
—For once I'd bought her some new underwear! cries the mother Charlotte.
I never buy her underwear. What's the point?
We rewear our old things. There's only the two of us, after all.
We don't need pretty things. To be clean is good enough.
Faded and run-resistant. Yellowed, run-resistant, and softened by repeated use suits us fine.
Our rounded bellies and our heavy thighs in the run-resistant outmoded styles.
That's good enough for us.
Run-resistant, shapeless,
and we're both contented.
No, I never buy her underwear!
Superfluous.
For once, I bought her underwear.
I should have known that something was up.
Wondered.
Suspected.
I was so trusting.

I was so sure that she was mine.
Fixed on me.
Tethered to me.
I thought.
My daughter.
My own daughter.
And now she's gone.
The story is not new.
She was capable of it.
She'd done it once before.
But I never thought.
She'd do it again.
I believed.
She'd been cured.
I do without love, I do.
I don't need a man.
A man in my house? No thank you!
—How happy we are, the women say, when the men are away.
It's Saturday, there'll be men in our midst.
Coming between us.
What a drag.
Never would I have taken off with a man. No and no.
But she did it. She did.
She left.
With a man.
That little idiot, she did it.
And I'd bought her underwear.
Why did I buy her underwear?
Why do all these girls need a man?
Weren't you happy with me, shouts the mother Charlotte.
Weren't you happy? Were we not happy?
You'd bring me milky coffee in bed each morning.

Were we not happy?
Were you not provided for, given everything you need?
Vegetables straight from the garden. Your food right on your doorstep. You can live here.
When so many people are struggling to get by.
You could live a life in your mother's house. Without going a-begging for your bread elsewhere.
The person in charge here, after me, is you.
And all the boarders of the boardinghouse, they also belonged to you.
We have a bathroom in the boardinghouse.
I have no idea why she left. I've racked my brain for a reason. I can't think of one.
Besides, we loved each other.
Now I'll have to hire some help to replace her.
Pay them.
And I shan't get along with my help.
My help won't work as hard as she did.
You and me, my girl, we worked well together.
And there's no denying that we made a good team.
From all points of view, it made sense: financially, our standards.
I've lost a great deal.
And I've tried very hard, but I can't make sense of your leaving.
It's been three weeks, and I am still hoping after you.
When I go out, my heart pounds at the slightest sight of you.
I see a figure in the distance, and I think it's you.
Naturally, it's not you.
From afar, I watch over the streets, the crossroads, the distances, the blurred horizons.
—No, says the police officer, no, madame, there's nothing we can do. It's not our concern.
A girl of twenty-six! Madame, it's not our concern.

At that age, madame, a girl is free to live her life.
At twenty, madame, your daughter would be guilty, but not at twenty-six years old.
It's no longer our concern.
And don't come shouting and crying in our office, it's very tedious and ridiculous.
—If only I did love him, wails Lili.
And she sobs.
But I don't love him, naturally.
I loved the young man from Transports.
I left because I was unhappy. But what's the point in saying so.
I'll not tell anyone that I was unhappy.
I'll keep it to myself.
My whole life.
And,
she cries.
I didn't leave with the man I loved.
I went off with the man I don't love.
I was unhappy.
I'm still unhappy.
Because it's like this.
I'm not lucky.
Everything goes the wrong way.
I don't know how happy people do it.
I wanted to make something happen.
I'd had enough. Enough.

ENOUGH

And so I left.
I swapped one master for another.

I won't tell him I was unhappy. I agreed to go away with him. He must believe that I did it for love.
I won't tell my mother that I was unhappy.
She wouldn't understand. She'd be hurt.
I won't tell anyone that I'm unhappy still.
I won't tell him,
I won't admit it to her.

UNHAPPY

Weren't you happy with me? cries the mother Charlotte.
Didn't you have everything?
She had everything.
Which is why, as Marthe and Élise chat in the doorway of the hotel, they spot the mother Charlotte on her way back from the police station, swaying from one side of the street to the other.
—Looks like she's been drinking.
She's in staggering search of her lost daughter.
—And why shouldn't I have been drinking?
She says this in a loud voice, out in the street with its face shuttered against the summer heat.
—I was thirsty, this hot weather is enough to make anyone thirsty. And I'm allowed to drink when I'm thirsty.
Everyone else does.
For once, I'll do the same as everyone else.
—I'd definitely say she's been drinking, says Marthe.
Come on, let's go in, I don't want to talk to her.
So the mother Charlotte keeps to her sorry path, in search of a vanished silhouette.
At least the boarders of my boardinghouse are good. They understand my situation. They're my friends. Thankfully, things can't

go wrong everywhere. This garment called life has more to it than just holes.

I wanted to get on with my life, cries Lili.
I do have the right to get on with my life.
Other people get on with their lives.
For once, I'll do the same as everyone else.
Did you not get on with your life?
Who hasn't got on with life?
I'll get on with my own life regardless.
She can get on with her life.
Let her get on with making her own life.
And making a life: it means going away with a man.
My life has been made.
She has made her own life.
—But what is she living on? cries the mother Charlotte.
Have you seen her? Either of you?
Give me any news.
If you see her, tell her about me.
And tell me about her.

Why did she do it?
But she'll die!
Now she's really losing it.
I lost my scarf.
Élise, have you seen my scarf? Marthe asks.
Is Maurice coming?
He left half an hour ago.
To get gas.
She's gone mad.
She'll die.
But why did she do it?
Élise shrugs her shoulders,
illusions shattered, hiding her face.
Oh well, I'll wear my aunt's scarf instead.
It's nighttime, cold white electric light illuminates the dining room of a provincial hotel, in the style of a train-station buffet.
A car engine cuts.
—Do they have a doctor with them?
They have a doctor, a friend of his, down from Paris.
Women are crazy.
She might have died.

—So, say the women, perched on the iron bed with the copper bed knobs in the bedroom filled with flowers. So, Lili, feeling any better?
They keep their voices low.
Lili: her face hollow, her eyes closed, lying flat under the blanket outlining the shape of her body.
—So, Lili, whispers Marthe.
Élise is crying.

—What a fright you gave us!
Lili smiles faintly, sighs.
—Don't move, you mustn't move.
After a silence, Marthe adds:
—We can't understand why you did this. A little one, a child, is such a beautiful thing.
Élise says the same with a nod of her head and the traces of tears on her cheeks.
—Maman, whispers Lili.
The two women exchange glances, their mouths full of questions. But the man enters the bedroom. He's holding medicine, a prescription.
—Let her be, he says,
and
Now's not the time for chatter,
and
You can come back later on.
He has a rough voice, curt, with a foreign accent.
It's not the voice of a hero from a novel.
His heavy manner has none of the lightness of a man who'd elope with a girl.
It's hard to imagine him killing himself over love.
And yet, this is the man who took Lili away.
Casually.
Just like that.
With his hard little sentences in his bad French.
He took her away, to this very bedroom. He found her a job (because they needed the money). Until yesterday, she was a sales assistant in a fabric store.

—Of course, Lili is insisting, of course we're still planning to get married.
—But why did you do it? You could have raised the child. You earn enough to raise a child.
Other people do.
—It's Maman, says Lili.
What would Maman have said if I'd had a baby out of wedlock?
Can't you understand, says Lili, Maman!
Her head is slightly raised, propped against a big pillow.
And projected onto the wall opposite, her eyes staring now (as if she were watching a movie at the cinema), she's imagining (as if she were reading a novel) a girl returning home, in shame, to her unpitying parents.
To a pitiless mother.
—What would Maman have said.
But, says Élise, then,
then she stops.
There is no but.
—I couldn't have done that to Maman.
I.
I don't know.
I couldn't stand the thought of it.
The two women say nothing. Because there's something in what she's saying that they can't understand.
—Well, at least you're alive, says Marthe.
That's the main thing.
—We *are* going to get married, will you be my witnesses?
Naturally, they'll be her witnesses.
—Are you happy? asks Élise with a stretched smile.
Yes, says Lili, I'm happy.

And her eyelids close like falling curtains.
I was afraid of what Maman would say about the baby.
—But you never see her anymore, says Élise. And anyway, a child always makes things right.
—Ah! says Lili, I didn't think of that, I forgot everything, I even forgot about the child, I didn't even think about it being a child, all I could think of was what she would say, and I was afraid.

The mother Charlotte went all the way to Nîmes.
Someone had given her their address.
Without daring to go and look, in a state of agitation, she'd stood on the corner of their street, hoping to catch a glimpse of Lili and that man.
But they didn't come.
Night fell without them.
The mother Charlotte returned home, having seen nothing, her gaze turned inward, her back bent over her heart.
And over every opinion she has of that man.
And over everything she'll say to that man when she sees him.
Words rising in her throat. Sentences. Answers preprepared.
And the questions.
It's that man whom her inward-looking eyes are addressing.
And time seems to fly by, the return journey passes so quickly, for the inner conversation is still ongoing when she arrives back at the boardinghouse.
The boarders are waiting up for her, they study her face, tense, immobile, their gazes the only signs of life in their stuffed bodies.
Waxworks.
The mother Charlotte goes up to her room.
She bids them good night. Did she bid them good night?
Yes, nods a jointed head.
No, thank you, she'll not have anything this evening.
To sleep.
(for want of death.)

The two things happened on the same day.
Because it's like this.
Always.

Two things, three things, four things happening, always, on the same day.
Two dreams, three dreams, four dreams shattering in a single minute.
There are so many dark days. So many days of sickness. So many days when death could come and no one would care.
So many waiting days.
Days of lost time.
Graveyard time.
So many days when chimeras are chimeras.
When life is just life.
Then, on one day amid all the others, they all burst into flame.
Chimera-life exults.
Today, the sun, so used to turning, stopped (or the earth did).
Suddenly, the dull gray life that everyone had grown accustomed to (for they had, after all)
ignites.
The Great Chicago Fire.
They'd given up. They'd accepted their dull habits.
But then, one day, everything changes.
Bitterness had set in.
Day after day.
They got used to it.
Since bitterness wants to live with us, we'll live with it.
A marriage of convenience.
But on this day, everything shakes.
Which is why, for the mother Charlotte as for everyone else, the two things happened on the very same day.

THE MAILMAN

—I'm long past hanging around for the mailman, says the mother Charlotte.

Don't give me your sentimental mailman stories.
I'll not listen. I couldn't care less about the mailman.
For one thing, I'll not go as far as the mailbox.
There's always someone to bring me the wine merchant's bill or the grocer's.
Why make the effort if it's just to receive my bills.
I've never received a letter in my life.
I mean a real letter.
And what's a real letter?
My life without letters.
Which is why, when an old woman dressed in gray wool entered the greenish-pink shade of my garden, my heart skipped a beat (though I didn't let it show).
For in her shriveled hand she was holding aloft the white envelope of a letter.
And it was a letter addressed to me.
I knew it before knowing it and realized without realizing it.
I was separating red currants from their stems with a little silver fork. I stopped.
—A letter, says the old woman, a letter!
and: my, it's hot today.
But it's cool in here—in your pantry. You've a nice spot for separating red currants from their stems with your little silver fork.
Then she wanders off, muttering to herself.
She mutters:
—I should have opened a boardinghouse, I should have done the same, with my fortune from a previous century.
For I would have enjoyed separating red currants from their stems with little silver forks in a refurbished old house under the cool heavy beams of a Gothic-style Provençal pantry.
She pauses to take a deep breath, regather her strength.
Then sets the gray of her woolen dress off against the green of a

low, leafy bower.
Meanwhile, the mother Charlotte, seated in the arched, whitewashed pantry, a copper basin gleaming in the shadows, turns and turns, weighs, measures, and studies the envelope containing her letter.
It's good-quality paper.
In my life, I will have received a letter.
And today is the day.
Carefully cutting along the edge, pulling out the four tiny pages, blackened by a slanting, clumsy, densely written hand.
Her face on fire.
Emotion coursing through her body.
Impatient, nervous, trembling, violent, reading it seated, reading it standing, reading it again, turning it over, refolding it, understanding nothing, reading a different letter (the one she'd been carrying about inside her, the one she was secretly waiting for), weeping, briskly wiping away a tear, a tear falling on the harried writing, a stain, a word blotted out. And the paper quivering in her clenched hand.
It is possible that there was some joy.
But a joy that hurts like a pain.
—That letter, the mother Charlotte told Marthe, it floored me.
For the letter arrived that morning and Marthe came by that afternoon.

POOR MARTHE

Because two things always happen at once.
Marthe came (despite the afternoon heat), acting mysteriously, her arms folded across her chest, her hands in her armpits gripping her kerchief. Silently, she walked up the garden path.

She knocked with her keys, not the knocker.
Everyone was resting after lunch.
The mother Charlotte leaned out from the balcony wound with morning glory.
Holding the letter of her life in her hand.
Poor Marthe is feeling very uneasy.
A burden.
If it weren't for the letter she'd received from Lili that morning, I wouldn't have come.
She says, timidly:
—Is this a good time?
How am I going to say what I have to say?
I'm coming down, go into the dining room.
The mother Charlotte comes downstairs, her heart beating hard, for she's now grasped that the second thing is about to happen.
What is it? Why is Marthe here?
Turning up while everyone is having their after-lunch rest.
—I'm coming down,
as if Marthe could still hear her.
—Take a seat, Marthe.
I received a letter from Lili this morning.
I wanted to tell you her news.
Marthe hesitates:
I thought you'd be pleased.
—So that's how it is, says the mother Charlotte, it's like that, is it, she makes no distinction between her mother and her friends?
I don't come first. I am not in top place; I'm ranked the same as a foreigner.
Her face ices over.
I'll never to be able to say what I've come to say, thinks poor Marthe.
Her face has closed.

—She told me she wrote you a letter.
—Indeed she has. She should have written a long time ago. But from what she wrote, it would have been better had she not written at all. For I might have been expecting a letter, but certainly not the one I received this morning.
Naturally, it was not the letter I'd been waiting for.
And don't play stupid when I'm talking to you.
The letter I have been reciting by heart for so many days—like a daily prayer—bears no resemblance to the letter I received this morning. My letter said: I'm coming home, forgive me, take me back, I was wrong, my life is so unhappy without you, I regret it, I await your reply. Instead I read: I'm fine, we're doing well. We. Who's we? I don't know we. Have you had your checkup at the dentist? I'll sign off with a sorry and hope to hear from you soon.
A sorry!
—She's a good girl, says poor Marthe, you mustn't blame her. It was always going to happen. She's pretty.
—Naturally, says the mother Charlotte, you take her side, you're for her, you take her part, you're the one who put these ideas into her head, you did this ...
—Oh oh says poor Marthe.
— ... everyone knows the kind of woman you are. Did you think it wasn't common knowledge? She'd never have left of her own accord.
Because in this story everyone is against me.
The whole world is against me, shouts the mother Charlotte.
Because I love my daughter.
Even if I didn't they'd still be against me.
Because everyone always takes against the woman on her own.
The woman on her own is always wrong.
She might have done things differently.
Other people find a thousand different ways and she could have chosen any one of them.

But she—the single woman—always manages to do things the only wrong way.
There are so many ways to love a daughter.
And how well she could have loved her daughter, that mother Charlotte.
There are thirty-six *right* ways.
(But she chose the thirty-seventh.)
—Naturally, screams the mother Charlotte, I'm wrong. I'm the one in the wrong. My daughter runs off in this nonsense manner and I'm the one who's wrong.
—I'm not saying that, says poor Marthe, that's not what I'm saying.
She draws closer, lowers her voice:
—She told me to tell you that they plan to move back here.
The mother emits an inarticulate sound. Blood rushes to her head.
The second thing, it's happening.
A chaos of thoughts.
—They're coming back.
She'll see her daughter again.
No, of course she won't live here at her mother's house but with her husband.
For Lili is married.
My daughter is married.
My daughter is married.
My daughter is married.
I am awaiting the man who took Lili away.
—What? How? says the mother Charlotte.
She never mentioned this in her letter.
He was working at the inn up on the main road—that's where they met.
He's got a bit of money.
The owners are moving to Marseille.
He bought the place off them, not outright, obviously.

He has big plans.
They'll be rich in a few years. That inn on the main road is in a good spot.
She's married well.
He's going to make something of himself,
murmurs poor Marthe.
But the mother Charlotte's face is still pale and drawn:
—It's not true, she hasn't married well, the joke's on you, stop this boasting. She's unhappy. The mother Charlotte knows when her daughter is unhappy.
I knew it this morning when I read her letter. I read it between the lines.
—Don't worry yourself unnecessarily, says poor Marthe.
—They are not worries, they are the facts.
Who'd run off believing in a man's promises nowadays? Empty words. Men are not to be trusted. We all know what they're like.
—I've never believed a single word a man has ever said, says the mother Charlotte. Not ME. And for that I congratulate myself.
Lili left a safe haven for an illusion.
When there's all that work to be done on a house, you can't make promises. And that inn on the main road bordered by plane trees is falling apart.
—They're planning to install a gas pump, says poor Marthe.
—So, he has the money for a gas pump, does he? If he's starting a restaurant he can't set up a garage. It's one or the other. He can't do both.
Because he's not so rich, is he? It's blackmail. I don't believe in his fortune. It's like something out of a novel. These foreigners who come here telling us that back home they lived like princes.
Well, I'm having none of it.
He'll get no help from me.
If my daughter is unhappy, she can come home, my door is open.

This is her home.
—Well, says poor Marthe, I hope it will all work out.
With time.
With the flowing water.
With the parting clouds.
With the drying tears.
With the wind to wipe them away.
With the changing seasons.
With the sliding months.
With the accumulating days.
With the lulling night.
With the cleansing rain.
With the new dead leaves.
With the new green leaves.
With time. With time. With time.
—Goodbye, says poor Marthe. I'll send little Gaston over with some peaches.
And quietly she slips away, quick and mysterious down the bright garden path.

A GALA MEAL

Under the leafy trees.
Striped twills, dark wools.
Heads leaning together.
Thin smiles.
Deviled eggs.
Everyone turns to look.
—Deviled eggs.
Muted exclamations.
—Deviled eggs.
Pass it on.
—Deviled eggs.
Brains.
A ring-shaped cake soaked in syrup.
Little pigeons.
Striped twills, dark wools, parasols, taffetas, long necklaces, and winged collars.
It's Sunday.
It's a very fine Sunday.
It's Lili's Sunday.
And from under the trees, through the open window: a glimpse of the long table set for lunch.
And bright flowers scattered over the spread tablecloth.
At the far end of the room, bustling around, the mother Charlotte, her shadow moving to the sounds of tinkling silverware.
—It's Sunday.
The old woman who'd sneaked into the pantry to put a piece of paper in the bin (a pretext) is calling from the doorway, her cupped hand a trumpet:

—Crayfish.
Everyone looks up, startled.
—Crayfish.
Heads pull apart.
—Crayfish.
Heads bobbing.
Scheming smiles. Toothy grins.
—Crayfish.
Stiff alpaca wools and winged collars.
—Now I shall ring, says the mother Charlotte, the Sunday lunch bell.
For it's my Sunday.
It's our Sunday.
It's Lili's Sunday.
The Sunday of deviled eggs, crayfish, and sorbet.
I'll watch the boarders of my boardinghouse shuffle past. Eyes down, mouths watering, noses pinched, throats tightening as they approach the festive table, the dining room filled to the rafters with frills, flowers, and bouquets.
And she rings the bell.
Her straw hat and the ribbon holding it steadily in place.
She rings and she rings and she rings.
All the boarders have come in.
But not Lili.
On the day of the lunch in her honor.
She rings and she rings and she rings.
And her hat on the gravel path where it fell and her hair come loose, strands growing damp (from the heat).
But still no Lili tardily opening the little gate at the end of the gravel path.
—Now I've broken the bell rope.
That Lili, who hasn't heard me ringing the Sunday lunch bell, the bell for deviled eggs.

The boarders dare not serve themselves. They look on in silence at the mother Charlotte, ringing and steadying, her eyes moist, her mouth wet.
—Start, says the mother Charlotte. I'll wait.
Heads bowed, smiles lowered, words withheld, gestures silent, shapes sketched in the air, grimaces, hand signals, unasked questions, ventured explanations, shrugged shoulders.
And at the far end of the table the mother Charlotte, frozen, a statue.
For Lili hasn't come.
—And she won't, cries the mother Charlotte.
She's not coming.
(It was all so lovely.)
I prepared the deviled eggs.
I made the crayfish, and the pigeon,
the little dishes, the sorbets,
the creams, the coffees, the chocolates,
and the sweets.
—BUT SHE'S NOT COMING wails the mother Charlotte.
Let night fall on the interminable meal and the stuffed boarders.
—Lili didn't come, shouts the mother Charlotte.
Lili didn't come.
—LILI DIDN'T COME, sobs the mother Charlotte, climbing up the stairs to her bedroom.
Will she come now?
Why didn't she come?
It was him. That man, he must have prevented her from coming.
For Lili, Lili would have come to see her mother who was expecting her.
That man is the guilty one.
Lili is the victim.
She'll come tomorrow.

I'll wait for her tonight.
I'll wait for her tomorrow.
And if each day the waiting continues, I'll add days to the days,
hours to the hours.
Waiting for my daughter,
who didn't come today.

—This life suits you, says the mother, you're happy.
—Yes, says Lili, on Sundays I go to the movies and in the evenings we have drinks with friends.
I won't tell her how every afternoon he goes out to play belote, leaving me all alone in the house.
—I'm happy, says Lili.
I won't tell her how I spend my time in the silent house shuffling a deck of cards, anxious to know the future, hoping my life will change. Dreaming of it. Wishing for it. For I don't know what kind of change.
Any change. Just as long as there is one.
—I'm happy, says Lili, at the roadside inn, on the main road bordered by plane trees, in time we'll be happy. The inn is in a good spot.
And now we're seeing each other again, Maman.
—If you keep spending money at the movies, says the mother Charlotte, your business won't last long.
I never go to the cinema, and if you recall, Lili, before you left neither did you. Neither you nor I ever went to the cinema.
Which is why my affairs are in good order.
As for going for drinks—no one ever made a profit doing that.
But if that is how you want to live your life, and you're happy,
if that's what you left me for, unfaithful daughter, if you married the movies, evening drinks, nights out, I'll say no more about it.
I've forgiven you, Lili, as you're well aware.
Because a mother always forgives her daughter.
I forgive you.

For Lili did come, in the end.
She didn't come on that sunny, long-prepared-for Sunday.
With the church nearby to sing us mass.

She didn't come on the day of elaborate ceremony, scented with celebration.
My deviled egg daughter, why didn't you come that day?

She came during the week.
An ordinary day.
Might have been a Tuesday.
Around three o'clock. Might have been ten to.
No one heard her come in.
The little gate made no sound.
And beneath her swift, soft-soled sandals, nor did the gravel path.

Like a pauper.
The dining room was empty.
The house silent.
The flowers and banners wilting and taken down.
From her balcony wound with morning glory, the mother Charlotte leaned out.
—Lili, it's you, she says. Come up, I'm coming down.
Their brows flushed, their eyes dark, they meet halfway up the wide staircase and exchange a shy kiss.
—Why didn't you come on Sunday? asks the mother, I had everything prepared.
What that mother Charlotte doesn't realize is that happiness never comes in the ways you want.
And today, once again, it's a delayed happiness. Happiness minus the grand setting. Happiness on its own. But still happiness. Happiness nonetheless.
—We're happy to see each other again, says Lili, isn't that what counts?
—I don't know why, says the mother Charlotte, but for me happiness needs an elaborate setting, a staging I can control.

It's as if I can't accept happiness as such.
I always have to make a fuss about it.
To tell you the truth, I was more concerned about the deviled eggs than I was about my daughter.
What's that coat you're wearing?
It doesn't suit you.
Did he choose it?
He thinks you look nice in that coat, does he?
Doesn't have much taste.
That hat isn't right for you.
And your shoes look cheap.
Where did you buy them?
From Prisunic?
—We don't have much money, says Lili, we're young, we're just starting out.
—I think I've aged, says the mother Charlotte, don't you think? I look older.
—We're all going to be happy now, says Lili, so soon you'll look younger.
The mother Charlotte chuckles.
Then,
—I have to go, my husband is working in the garage. There's no one minding the café.
—He was the one who stopped you from coming on Sunday.
—Why would you say that? says the daughter. I told you, the previous owners—we were expecting them on Saturday night, but instead they came on Sunday morning.
—Ah, says the mother Charlotte, I wouldn't put it past him. After all, he kidnapped my daughter.
—He understands me, says Lili, he knows what a mother is, he has nothing against us seeing each other. On the contrary. We moved here so that I would be happy.

My little Maman.
—Oh, says the mother Charlotte, shrugging her shoulders, what good are words.
You left me. You're happy without me. You don't need me anymore.
She doesn't need me anymore.
I've been replaced.
Daughters are divorcing their own mothers now, are they.
I turned down marriage proposals when you were little, Lili. For your sake.
The love I felt for you left no room for any other love.
And I didn't miss it—that other kind of love.
You were the replacement.
Off she goes, scurrying away.
In a hurry to come. In a hurry to leave. In a hurry to get the visit over with.
Sneakily, like a forbidden lover.
—When will you be back? calls the mother.
—I don't know, replies Lili, but I'll come.
—Stay for a while longer, have something to drink, to eat, you haven't had anything to drink.
—Thank you, but I can't.

Slowly, slowly, things return to normal. Without incident.
The mother Charlotte glimpsed the man from a distance. She grows accustomed to seeing his outline, his foreigner's face.
A Slav, murmurs the mother Charlotte, a Slaaav.

Once, at dusk, she went up to the big road and its ribbon of plane trees.
They came face-to-face by the gas pump.

Lili watching from the doorstep.

At that moment, appearing on the crest of the hill, silhouetted against the sky: the classical image of the shepherd and his soft flock of sheep.

—It's you, says the mother Charlotte.

The son-in-law doesn't reply; he's serving a customer.

It's not that serving requires all his attention. He keeps out of family dramas.

—So it's you.

It is him, indeed.

Never would the mother Charlotte have gotten herself tangled up with such a boy.

Absolutely not.

and:

I wonder what Lili sees in him.

—I'll never understand! Shouts the mother Charlotte. NEVER.

Don't shout like that, out here on the main road, says Lili, people will talk.

Go home.

All the restaurant fittings are brand new.

The little tables. The bar. The mirrors. The ceiling lamps.

—You'll go bankrupt, says the mother Charlotte.

—Don't wish ill on others, replies Lili.

And Marthe. The baby Marthe's cradling.

Lili takes him in her arms.

He's the same age as hers would have been. She loves the baby.

She carries him, she talks to him, she smiles at him. Yes, she'll give him a chocolate, an orange. Does he like chocolate? Does he like oranges?

Yes, they'll walk down to the Rhône river. Want to? Yes, he wants to.

—You'll go bankrupt, shouts the mother Charlotte.

She's stuck at the same place in the conversation.

—And how's your building work coming along? asks Marthe.
So what if the mother Charlotte started on some construction work while Lili was gone, to take her mind off her sorrows? That's no one else's business.
—Very well, she says.
Stay and have dinner with us? asks Lili.
—My boarders will be expecting me.
I'll not dine here. Ah no.
I'll not eat at his table. Ah no.
She leaves.
And the others gaze out at the bright hole of night through the swing door.

THE ROSE BUSHES

The mother Charlotte, pruning roses in the garden.
In the morning, at around ten o'clock.
Like Dr. Grumberg's mother.
Wearing the same hat with the broad ribbon.
Wearing gloves.
Holding pruning shears.
Like the doctor's mother.
The doctor's mother was a great lady.
And this morning, in the resting sun, the mother Charlotte is a great lady.
A Lady of the Manor.
As Lili's husband passes by on the path.
He spies Lili's mother pruning roses on this brand-new day.
He thinks:
That's Lili's mother.
Lili is my wife.
I'll say hello to my wife's mother.

He pushes the gate open, the gravel shifts.
He approaches the mother Charlotte.
The mother Charlotte is pruning the garden roses.
He coughs.
He drags a foot.
He holds nothing against this woman.
Only good will.
After some time, the mother Charlotte, busy with her different actions, lifts her head to look up at the waiting man.
—I didn't see you there, she says,
Then resumes her work.
With gusto.
—Greetings, says the man.
She doesn't reply.
—Greetings Maman, the man says again.
Which was the last straw.
—I see you're not working this morning, says the mother Charlotte.
Everyone has to work, *I'm* working.
I'm pruning these roses.
—I had an errand to run, says the man.
—So you leave Lili to work while you take a stroll, says the mother Charlotte.
The man starts to reply, but holds back.
She's Lili's mother.
Lili is his wife.
—Ah, he says, pretending to laugh, no, that's not it, but I spotted you pruning the roses in the garden, so I wanted to stop and say hello.
The mother Charlotte pricks herself on a thorn:
—Naturally, she says, you've come to look over your inheritance.
—Ah, says the man, still pretending to laugh, you're joking.
—I'm not dead yet, she shouts.
I don't even want to die.

The man is at the gate.
He's shouting back:
—Goodbye, till next time, when this'll go better.
For he truly wants things to be better.
—In time, says Lili, we'll all be happy.
In time, with time, with the passing seasons, with the yearly celebrations, with dusks layering upon dusks, with the waking of each new morning.
With the days separated from their stalks.
With time. With time. With time.

—You'll have to speak more clearly, says the mother Charlotte, I can't understand a single word you're saying.
He doesn't know how to speak French.
He's not French is he.
—Have some more chicken (says Lili) since you've finally come to my house. Do help yourself, Maman. You're in your daughter's home.
—I'm in my daughter's home, but I'm not hungry, shouts the mother Charlotte.
If you think I'm hungry, you're mistaken.
Have you seen how your husband eats?
Look at him, Lili, please. Love's making you blind.
Where was he raised? To behave like this at the table!
He's eating his meat with his fingers.
—What are forks for? says the mother Charlotte, speaking across the silence of the table,
conducted by the tinkling of cutlery, the wine being poured, the mouths in motion.
The man stops chewing, he hadn't heard what she said, he glances at Lili.
—This chicken, says Lili, trying to repair things, is not so easy to cut with a knife.
Now he understands.
The mother Charlotte eats her meat in tiny bites.
—At the boardinghouse, she says, everyone has good table manners.
And I always taught you to have good table manners, Lili.
Never forget that you married a well-brought-up girl.
The man has stopped eating. He is silent.
—Eat, shouts Lili.
—If you think I'm hungry, says Lili's husband, you're mistaken.

He pushes his plate away.
But says nothing to the mother Charlotte.
—Are people not very talkative in your country, says the mother Charlotte.
The man says nothing. He'll not say a word.
The mother Charlotte is Lili's mother. Lili is his wife.
He loves Lili therefore he respects the mother Charlotte.
He knows what a mother is.
Over the plate he pushed away, he's thinking of his own mother, a vision distant in space and time, his mother whom these two have never met … Kind eyes wrinkled by love and the passing of the years.
He swallows a sigh. He had no choice but to leave her. Children have to get on with their lives. Mothers stand at the threshold of the home, to watch their children leave. It's destiny. Even so, children never forget their mothers (and mothers never forget their children).
Now he's no longer thinking of his own mother, he's looking across at the mother Charlotte, he wants to be good for the mother Charlotte. With a clumsy gesture she's just dropped her fork on the floor, so he hastens to pick it up.
—There's no point in trying to be nice, shouts the mother Charlotte. I've no use for your niceties.
He took my daughter away, now he wants to be nice.
Gallantry, if you please.
—I don't need his gallantry, shouts the mother Charlotte.
—In his country, says Marthe, they say the men are extremely courteous.
—Naturally, you Marthe, you take his side. You've got your eye on him. We all know what you're like. The great defender of all men. Don't look so put out, you're the same age as my daughter.
I can say what I like to you. Don't come sticking your nose into Lili's marriage.

—Tread carefully around your mother! shouts Marthe,
and goes out to join Lili in the kitchen.
She's getting more and more out of control.
—You think, says Lili, wiping away a tear with the back of her hand as a second one slides down onto the plates.
She's washing up some dessert plates and glasses because they don't have enough for the last course.
Élise, her husband, the baby, and Marthe have joined them for dessert, liquors, coffee.
—You think, says Lili, her hands busy drying plates with a fresh dish towel from the dresser.
You think, and because she can't hide the pain in her face, because she doesn't have a free hand to dry her tears, she turns her pained face and her sorrow to Marthe who looks at her with alarm.
—You think, and she shrugs her shoulders, making circles with her cloth on the gleaming plate.
I was so happy that we were all going to be eating together.
I believed in it.
I was so happy.
I thought: at last she's come to her senses.
I prepared everything so that she'd be happy.
I don't know what else to do (she exclaims in a low voice).
I don't know what else we can do.
Her arms dangling, the cloth in her hand.
There's nothing to be done.
—Come now, says Marthe, don't get so upset, and she takes the cloth to finish the drying.
Lili turns her face away, for now Élise's husband has come into the kitchen to rinse the little rubber rabbit that the baby had just thrown on the floor.
—At least I came, the mother Charlotte is saying to Élise, who's sitting beside her.

A daughter is always forgiven.
In the end, you accept it.
All mothers go through something like this, says the mother Charlotte,
—Of course, of course, murmurs Élise, and stretches forward to set her glass, containing a last drop of cassis, down on the table. And we're so happy for Lili. Truly happy.
Families love each other. Things always work out in the end.
—Why yes, yes they do, chuckles the mother Charlotte softly.
She holds out her glass to Lili's husband.
—I'll have a bit more of that delicious cassis, my son-in-law, she says.
Marthe and Lili come back to the table with the coffee and the cups.
—Join us, says the mother Charlotte, cheerfully. What were you two up to out there? Aren't they chatty! Making up stories. They could write a novel, those two. Pour me a little more of that liquor, my son-in-law.
—Come here, Lili, come closer to me.
You'll drink your liquor next to me.
She draws up a chair, and as Lili sips her cassis, the mother Charlotte wraps her arms around her.
Smiles. Enjoyment. Relaxation.

At that very moment, the shepherd is passing by on the main road.
They see him walking slowly past the open windows, bright with cacti and geraniums.
Lili shakes off her mother's embrace and rushes to the window.
Leaning out over the flowers, she hails him with her voice and a wave.
The shepherd turns off the road and comes up to the house.
Someone finds him a chair.
Let him drink a glass of cassis with us.
—All that's missing now is a baby, someone says.

—Like this one, adds Élise.
—If only there were a grandchild! says the mother Charlotte in a serious voice.
—You'd dote on him, cries Maurice, Élise's husband.
—Why of course I would, replies the mother Charlotte, smiling. (her face tinged purple from the liquor and the end of the meal.)
Naturally, I'll be a doting, dotty grandmother.
I'll be the kind of grandmother who's dotty about her grandchild.
Look how she dotes on him, how dotty she is about him, that's what everyone will say.
We've never seen a grandmother like it.
She's just crazy about the little one.
Naturally, says the mother Charlotte, I'll go dotty over the little one.
—I'd like for us to have a little girl, says Lili, I'll name her Claude.
Her husband gives her a sympathetic look.
He knows that since her illness Lili can no longer have children.
Lili knows it, too. Still, she repeats what she said, with tender feeling:
—A little girl, Claude, a little redhead.
—I love Claude, says Marthe, it's a pretty name.
And over the sparkling glasses, the carafes of liquor, they toss girls' names between them like bouquets of flowers:
Marinette, Ghislaine, Nadine, Verveine, Corinne, Juliette.
They call out to each other, they're having fun.
And Lili grabs hold of Élise's baby excitedly, kissing him effusively, entertaining him as if he were her own.
(I know I can't have children, but let me amuse myself.)
—I love them both! cries Lili to Marthe, who pretends not to hear.
We could all be so happy together.
All I want is for us all to get along.
For things to be easy.
Me, says Lili, I'm on the side of peace.
—You can't have peace in a family, says Marthe.

If it's not one thing, it's another, and don't think you're the only one.
—I love them both! shouts Lili.
Naturally I love the both of them. I've grown attached to my husband.
—But your mother! shouts Marthe.
—Maman loves me, says Lili, it's because she loves me.
I can't hold it against her. I understand her.
—And you'll live your whole life not knowing whose side to take—your mother's or your husband's.
We'll speak of this again one day.
Lili, irritated, shouts:
—Why is it so hard to talk to you, then adds, a bit nastily: it's because Henri left you, isn't it.
Marthe is silent, she turns away, she's hurt.
Without looking at Lili, she goes out through the back, into the courtyard.
Lili remains alone in the bar, then goes out the front, into the square.
Behind her, the hotel lobby, empty, ugly, communal, sad, dusty, cheap, dead.
Like the little quarrels between women.

> Quarrels.

I'm going to invite them back here for a meal.
In this story, we go from meal to meal.
This family saga shall advance through the years from feast to feast, silverware to silverware, fine tableware to fine tableware, crushed flowers to explosions of flowers.
—What do you say, Marthe, says the mother Charlotte, they invited me, I'm going to invite them back here for a meal. I'm going to show that man that in France we know a thing or two about good manners. I'm going to teach him how to host, since he doesn't know how. I'm going to teach him a lesson.

He has no idea what kind of family he's married into. Not a clue.
He has married into a family that knows how to host a dinner.
—As a matter of fact, says the mother Charlotte, I wanted to know if your pomegranates are ripe.
That's why I came.
I've one or two ripe ones but not enough to fill a basket, I'll add some nectarines if you like.
I'll walk them over this afternoon.
We'll go and take a look at my building work.
After big family meals, the lady of the house always proposes a little outing.
Let's go to the park, walk up to the castle, it's not far.
Walking in little groups to the sounds of idle chatter and light laughter on the bright path.
—Is it going well, the construction work on the villa? asks Marthe.
—Naturally, replies the mother Charlotte, I know how to get things done.
If my daughter hadn't left me.
She'd be overseeing it all.
The mistress of my new house.
She'd have what she'll never have with that boy.

But family meals can turn

>   on a screw
>   on a nail
>   on a word.

In a single blow, the whole meal upended.
The tablecloth in a tangle and plates turned upside down.
No one saw it coming.
They imagined they were attending a special meal to mark a baptism, a communion, a wedding, a housewarming, a pardon, a return, a new beginning.

We put so much faith in such meals.
It's how we express our family feelings, our bonds: through the rituals of eating together.
It was all going so well.
The sun was in no hurry to set. It was gilding the ribbon of road where the peaceful family groups were taking an after-dinner stroll.

But then there was a screw.
A brand-new screw.
Newly screwed into a brand-new wall.
Lili's husband said:
—If I were you, I'd have that screw screwed in a little bit farther along.
And the mother Charlotte's heart blasted open, knocked over the vases of flowers, flipped the laden tablecloth.
—I knew it.
I thought it.
I was sure of it.
I suspected it.
I said it.
He thinks it's his.
He thinks he owns it. My house.
It was for the inheritance. That's why he married my daughter.
You don't need a high school diploma to work that out.
My beautiful new villa, white and Provençal, dazzling in the sun.
He thinks it belongs to him.
Naturally. Why not?
No, don't bother.
Well, let him give up his son-in-law's schemes of a villa, white and Provençal, high on the hill.
He made a mistake.
My clear crystal villa in the high sun.
Give them up.
The mother Charlotte will not allow herself to be robbed
duped
played
drawn

withdrawn
diminished
stripped.
He chose the wrong family.
—You'll get nothing from me, screams the mother Charlotte.
There's nothing here for you.
Not even that screw.
This isn't your house. This isn't your home.
You have no say here. I'm the one in charge.
This is my house.
Let me spell it out for you: my many-windowed villa, my undoored troubadour villa, ritornelle, pimpernel, light and skies, sun, fireflies, lace and shade, olives, cicadas, thrushes and vines, sun, sun, sun and Occitan, the Tarasque of Tarascon, the castle, the mistral
                                               none of it belongs to you,
not even that screw.
He's been making plans, arrangements.
He's been imagining.
He's been giving orders.
And me? What am I? Who do you take me for?
I'm the old woman.
That's what you're thinking, admit it.
We'll soon be rid of the old woman.
The old woman.
The old mother Charlotte.
You can't fool me, screams the mother Charlotte.
I'm not some old woman you can fool.
You've made a big mistake. They're not very intelligent where you come from, are they?
I'm from a good race.
I'm from a good generation.
You young ones can't fool us,

Our generation can hold its own.

There's more intelligence in my wrinkles than in the color in your cheeks monsieur my son-in-law.

As for my light house, for my bright house, as for my house so beautiful and bright and light—so white, wide, and Provençal, in the sun among the pinked firs, the chestnut trees, the silver date palms, the tiny bits of gravel in the path (for everyone is a part of the party here), amidst the stunted, the parched, the twisted, the châteaus cracked by time, the shut shutters, the flat roofs, the vipers, the cypress trees, the villages of Mazargue and Camargue, the sun so yellow, Picasso, Prévert in the bright white glare, figland and scrubland…

Put it all together, mix well, pour over a sauce made of sunshine and there you have it: Provence. For today is the day of our big family meal and at the blue heart of the heat stands my large opal house, which shall never be yours.

Naturally, I did the opposite to other people. The meal I intended to mark a new beginning, an agreement, a union, a future, a clarity, turned out to be for a break-up, for pain, for severance, for mourning, for death.

I'm the kind of person who hosts a big dinner for when everything is being torn apart.

—Come away now, says the man, come.

He's speaking in a low voice, guiding Lili out into the bright white stain of the outdoors. He's tugging at her sleeve.

Come, says the man, I can't stand her any longer. It's too much. It's too much.

And with his full male voice, he howls a great sound, it reverberates through the empty, freshly painted, freshly constructed house, with no doors.

And the mother Charlotte pales. She's afraid.

For a man's voice is a man's voice.

The sound of a man frightens the mother Charlotte. Without understanding what he's saying, she thinks to herself: perhaps I went too far.
He's tugging his wife away by the arm, and shouting:
—It's too much.
He'll never set foot in her house again.
She can keep her ice-villa in the sun, its reflection bouncing off the white coast and its scattered olive trees.
Rest easy, shouts the man.
It's over. FINISHED.
He has never known a woman to be so mean, so bad, his voice reverberating and bouncing out of the freshly tiled entrance hall.
On the step, looking out at the spread of white, Lili is crying.

He is dragging his wife along the hot road in the shadowless evening.
He is shouting:
—You'll have to choose, it's me or her.
—She's my mother, sobs Lili, I choose my mother.
—Naturally, Lili, she is your mother, and it's a great shame, but if you want to see her again, you'll have to do it without me there.
A separation, Lili. This evening, I broke up with my mother-in-law.
He cracks a match. He lights a cigarette, leaning forward, cupping his hands around his mouth.
He's a man.
And this evening he's fighting.
This troubled evening.
This tormented evening.
This tearful evening.
This cigarettes evening.
Lili is crying.
He hates to see Lili cry.

And so he gets angry.
—She's crying! If he were breaking up with her, there'd be fewer tears, he's sure of that.
He's known it for a long time.
He worked that one out a long time ago.
He is silent. Because when have words ever fixed anything. The people who chatter on are never the most intelligent.
He thought he'd found a family. A family-in-law.
—She welcomed you, cries Lili, she made asparagus for you. She welcomed you in warmly.
—That's it, shouts the man's muffled voice, defend her, defend her. She hurt you, you told me. She destroyed your life once before. She'll do it again, believe me. If someone hurts you once, they'll do it again, always, remember that Lili.
—You don't know what you're talking about, cries Lili and blows her nose.
—Defend her, shouts the man, don't bother about me, go back to her house, don't stay with me if your heart's not in it.
—You're crazy, says Lili.
Speaking his backward sentences, words in the wrong order, making mistakes, he says calmly:
—With your mother you always have to give her hell.
He says this quietly into the bluing night, he thinks "give her hell" is a polite way of saying "argue with." It's what he was taught.
They come to the road bordered by plane trees. In pale shadows the mass of the solitary inn emerges from deep within the landscape.
He drops words along the main road on this night thick with the sounds of lovers kissing, all the lovers in the world. But now is not the time for tenderness. It is the hour of severance.
The key turns in the lock, the door creaks, lights switch on.
And between the sounds of dishes being washed joylessly, gleamlessly, amid the noises of their evening meal: separation, rancor, bit-

terness, complaint, imprecations, regrets, memories, disappointed hopes, woes.

Tonight, over at the main plant, they reduced the strength of the electric current.

And the faint glow of yellow light throws shadows of the couple's weary gestures onto the wall.

The gestures of clothes falling to the floor, dresses lifted braces down, blankets kicked off, backs turned, bodies divided.

Nightfall.

It's since we went to the villa, murmurs Lili.
I'll always remember,
coming home.
Naturally, I still visit her.
I make sure to get away once a week.
I don't tell my husband.
I leave quietly.
Unnoticed, I leave.
Furtively.
I glance to the left, to the right.
I wait till he's busy.
I tell him I'm going to your house, or to the butcher's, or to Élise's, or to the market.
And when I'm there I don't sit down. I don't have time.
I refuse the tea and the little cakes she offers me.
I tell her I'm in a hurry.
I perform. I smile, I pretend to be relaxed.
I tell her that business is good,
that I'm in charge and mustn't stay away for too long,
that it's against my best interests to stay with her, but I'll stay for a little while just to prove I'm willing to go against my best interests.
And I smile, I smile, I smile.
But I don't want to smile.
For it's like this:
We are living with our elbows planted on tables, our heads bowed, heavy in our upturned hands. Our mouths despondent, our eyes anxious in our weary faces.
—Right, says Marthe, speaking out of one corner of her half-painted mouth. Right.
But we all have our troubles. Wouldn't you say?

she raises her head slightly, her features redrawn:
—Wouldn't you say? All of us: we set off with our hopes, our passions, our loves, but before long here we are, planting our elbows on café tables.
She glances around her:
—In the style of a train-station-buffet.
then:
still, I should probably give them a wipe.
—Whenever I visit her, says Lili, it's always the same tune:
He's keeping you from coming, he's the one who, he only married you for.
And when I get home, it's the same old song from him.

THE VERB TO CHOOSE

And now, cries Lili, now I have to choose. They both keep telling me the same thing. But choose what?
—If you loved him as much as I loved Henri you'd know who to choose.
—Choose, shouts Lili.
                              but why?
I need them both.
Mother and husband.
There's no way I can choose between them.
Why should I have to choose?
I don't know how.
I'm only a woman.
I won't abandon my husband.
I won't abandon my mother.
I don't want to cause either of them that sorrow.
—Sorrow will come along all by itself, says Marthe, don't you worry about that.

—Who am I supposed to choose? I've a thousand reasons to choose and not to choose, I'm losing my mind.
Marthe sings, mockingly: "maybe I'm wrong
maybe I'm right …"
—You're teasing me, murmurs Lili, but it's not funny. Do you know how? How to make a choice, in life?
You keep telling us the story of your great love affair with Henri, but he left and you didn't go after him, you didn't go looking for him, and now you live with your husband as if nothing ever happened. The choice presented itself and you chose nothing.
Show me a woman who's chosen something.
Some women choose one fabric over another, but fabrics fade and market sellers keep selling just so that women can tell themselves they've made a choice in their lives.
But for my part, I'll not choose, cries Lili.
—Fine, says Marthe, since she won't choose, life will choose for her. Life takes care of itself and there's no point in us getting in a state over problems we can't solve.
Because they solve themselves without us.
Because life, it lives on its own momentum.
It goes on, all by itself.
It doesn't need us to help it along.
No plan, no calculation, no prediction, nothing, nothing has ever made a difference.
So Lili is wrong to torture her heart over the verb "to choose."
Life takes care of the choosing. It's life that decides.
for:
They all knew that war had been declared, a new kind of war, patent pending.
Everyone knew that deportation had been invented, a new make of deportation, patent pending.
And barbed wire,

a new style of barbed wire;
and hanging,
custom-made;
and graveyards,
a new make and a new turnover;
and in a grieving sky, where the blue had turned to black,
paint and supplies,
a prize-winning no-nonsense new make,
a new god,
a peerless new model
beating all the competition.
Loveless.
Bloodless.
The whole world knew it.
A new death.
Incomparable.
Rendering the old style, with its scythe and its cape and its wasted eyes, obsolete.
For in the new world,
everyone gets the same make,
Men are skeletons and death has color in its cheeks, a wide girlish grin and big, laughing, loving, shining eyes.
Because we've grown tired of the old world.
And we've received delivery of a brand-new world,
stamped, signed, read, and approved.
Everyone knew it.
When they came for Lili's husband, the new make of police officer, revised and corrected, authorized, let-them-pass,
everyone knew it.
Which is why, standing erect in the hotel doorway, Élise and Marthe are watching the stooped figure of Lili's husband, whom Lili is accompanying to the police station.

On his convict's back he's carrying his clogs and a brown wool blanket for tomorrow.
—He was supposed to be there at nine o'clock, says Marthe.
Élise sniffs:
—It's still sad though, she says.
—I was right, says Marthe.
The choice gets made.
There was no need for Lili to get herself in such a state over choosing.
The choice takes care of itself.
The choice doesn't need us.
—Maybe he'll come back, says Élise.
Why would he come back?
Who gets to stay? Who gets to return?
And
Better if he didn't.
And in a whisper:
Do you think Lili will mind?
—Well, her mother won't at any rate, Élise replies.
And together they turn to go back inside, the man in the distance having faded from view, en route to the fantastic holiday resort of tomorrow.
New make, one-size-fits-all.

They're bending over their work, pretending to be busy with cleaning, when Lili comes up to the bar.
—A white wine, she says.
She doesn't seem too upset, the women say.
How is a woman, who has just handed her husband, whom she has never cheated on, over to the people who'll transport him to Dachau, to behave?
—A white wine, Lili says.
She's not crying, the women think.

Doesn't misfortune make a person cry?
And
Time will tell if it is a misfortune.
Her hands are steady and she's drinking straight.
Doesn't despair make a person tremble?
She's numb, think the women, it hasn't registered yet, she hasn't understood.
—So, says Marthe, hitting the silence with her lively voice and the flat of her hand, you left him there?
Lili raises her head, ponders a moment before replying:
—I had no choice, she says, he didn't want me to stay.
What did you think it was? A salon, a boudoir, a place for delicacies and tender words?
—No, of course not, replies Marthe, but we said to ourselves, we thought, we believed, we expected, we'd imagined, Élise had supposed, and I, I'd said.
—You were wrong, says Lili, I left him there. With only his eyes, which are the color of fear.
This season's color! It suits everyone.
A new shade. It just gets better and better.
There was another man there, says Lili.
His eyes were this season's color too.
—You don't seem too upset, says Marthe.
Lili empties her wineglass, sets it down with a small brisk gesture. She says:
—Oh!
And that's all she says because

>   she is not thinking about what Dachau is.
>   she is not at any personal risk of being deported;
>   she's been released from her marriage and it's a great
>   gust of air beneath a heavy sky;

nevertheless, her feelings have been fittingly, delicately affected.

      And every effort will be made to get him out of there.
—Oh!, with a small catch in her voice.
Nothing else.
Then she simpers:
—Things never happen to me the way they do to other people. My life,
it's a whole novel.

MY TURN!
SHOUTS THE MOTHER CHARLOTTE

I'll not miss my turn, not when my daughter is at stake.
The enemy is away, let's make the most of it.
Let's make the most of the adversary's despair.
And the bad luck he's been served.
Thank goodness I didn't leave and he didn't stay.
Thank goodness the roles have now been reversed,
swapped back to their correct positions.
It's a stroke of luck and without luck what would we do?
—What is luck? asks the mother Charlotte.
He was unlucky, says Léa (the shepherd's mother).
Look, here I am pruning my roses—just as I was on that first morning he spoke to me, says the mother Charlotte.
The same bright morning light,
the same sunshining of the wet lawn,
the same birdsong and the same birds.
I have the same pruning shears.

Naturally, it's all a matter of luck.
—I've never had any luck either, says Léa.
Good fortune has always passed me by.
I'll die without knowing happiness.
Léa lifts the heavy wet laundry basket high onto her shoulder.
She's on her way home from the washhouse by the river.
—You remember, she says, when Julien was sick.
—You should have brought your wheelbarrow, the mother Charlotte replies.
—Bah, Léa sighs, but she can't turn her head because of the basket.

Didn't even think to bring my wheelbarrow—that's how unlucky I am.
She mutters on to herself as she walks away:
sadness is not so hard to bear if you're used to it, it's just an ordinary day.
It's happiness I couldn't cope with, she shouts, turning her whole body back around to face the mother Charlotte.
Just the thought of happiness, it makes me feel sick with dizziness.
But Charlotte can no longer hear her and Léa is shouting only for the stones and the branches overhanging the track. (who are listening attentively)

The mother Charlotte is in the pantry. She's shelling dry beans.
Tightening their woolen scarves around their shoulders, a few elderly women have come to help.
The pantry is in the shape of a church, one or two ancient candlesticks stand on the dark wooden shelves.
—You're very lucky to be sheltering in my house during wartime, says the mother Charlotte, I can keep you fed.
—We'll show our gratitude, say the old women, shaky and anxious, nervous and sticky-sweet.
You know that nothing is for nothing.
—I know, I know, says the mother Charlotte, then casts her eye over her old women.
You're dropping beans on the floor, she says, now is not the time to waste a bean.
She glances through the narrow window in the shape of a cross; the mistral is up.
And my poor girl, she murmurs, all alone up on the main road bordered by plane trees, an empty house is a lonely place these days.
The old women sigh.

—Yes, says the mother, alone, isolated, far away, up on the main road, my daughter. It can't go on like this.
I'll not tolerate it any longer.
It has to change.
—She can't stay up there by herself, say the old women, so alone, with the years racing by.
And with everything else racing by. On those big roads.
The motorists.
Telling themselves they're living a great adventure just because they're at the wheel of a car on an open road, as far as the eye can see.
—In my day, says an old woman, we didn't drive on roads merged with the sky.
(the young are thirsty for adventure.)
Lili isolated
Lili desolated.
—Something's not right, says Lili, I'm antsy, I feel uneasy tonight.
And the nights roar with motorists.
I'll close the garage.
The restaurant is more than enough.
My husband'll forgive me if I can't keep the business running as well as he did. I'm only a woman.
When he gets back, he'll find his business has shrunk a little, but he'll forgive me.
His return.
—Upon his return, he'll forgive you, says the shepherd. He'll be so happy to be home.
—Naturally, the return, says Marthe.
—Return (Élise).
—I'll not leave this house, there's no way, says Lili. It's my husband's house and for as long as the war is on, I'll do his work for him, as so many other women are doing.

I'll not abandon this house, my husband shall have his business to come back to.

Upon his return.

And we'll all be so happy.

—Of course, say Marthe and Élise in chorus.

They've brought their knitting with them, to pass the afternoon. They're sitting under the large chestnut tree overhanging the garage, in the shade.

—I am my husband's wife, says Lili.

—No one is saying otherwise, says Marthe.

—He can trust me, cries Lili.

Then abruptly she turns away, her cheeks flushed pink.

—Look, here comes Maman.

—Hello my daughter, says the mother Charlotte tenderly, I'm so happy to see you.

It makes me sad to think of you here.

isolated desolated.

It keeps me awake at night.

—As you can see, says Marthe, we've come to keep her company.

—And it's so much work for you, my daughter, the upkeep of this house, you're growing thin.

Can't you see how much thinner she is?

—You worry too much, says Marthe.

The shepherd moves off, soundlessly.

And Lili comes back with a chair for her mother.

The mother Charlotte sits down, levels her chair in the gravel:

—Lili, you can come home. In my house, you're at home.

I've brought a parcel for your husband.

Yes, I help prepare parcels for her husband.

—When will all this be over? the women wonder.

—I'm spending a fortune! shouts the mother Charlotte.

—I'm happy, says Lili, that you all here.

I need you.

I don't feel so uneasy anymore. I'm happy. I'm forgetting my husband. I'm forgetting I even have a husband.
And I'm forgetting he's been deported.
Completely.
Your company is all I need to make me happy.
Let's make some coffee.
The women laugh.
—I'm so happy, says Lili,
neither desolated
nor isolated.
But this evening will come to an end and soon you'll be on the road full of shadows.
And I'll stay here
>isolated
>desolated
watching you go.
Because I can't stay here all alone! Lili shouts.
I can't beaaaaaarrrr solitude.
I can't help it.
I get frightened when I'm all alone.
I'm frightened. I'M FRIGHTENED
of everything, of nothing: the shadows, the creaking woodwork, the squeaks, the silences.
I am sick with fear.
I need to be with you.
I need to talk.
I need to hear you talking.
To hear real voices, real sounds.
Now they've left, smudged into the shadows of the road, and I hardly dare go back inside.
I close the door carefully.
I go into my living room. Fearfully.
I check behind the furniture and I draw the curtains. I keep my eyes

closed that I won't see the scary shadows through the windows that could be lying in wait for me.
When will this be over?
I hate solitude, says Lili, addressing the silence of the room.
She talks to herself these days.
She says it again, quieter: I hate solitude.
Then she drops a pair of scissors. She stirs a pan, making it ring.
She opens the door of the side cabinet, it creaks.
I don't like solitude because, for me, solitude is night.
Helen Keller.
I am no longer alive. I can feel myself dying.
I see nothing. I hear nothing. I don't say a word.
I don't like solitude.
And when there's no one here to talk to, I'm startled to find that I have no speech left inside. I don't feel anything anymore.
And yet I love my mother, I love my husband, I love my friends.
But my heart only works in contact with other hearts.
Alone, I can't function. It's like being in a coma.
A coma is a predeath.
But I'm not the kind of heroine who relishes death, calling it Solitude.
People who have that taste for death, for stopping life, leave me cold.
On my own I lose my head and my heart, and without them who am I?
I can only live in a group. Don't talk to me about solitude.
And she wipes away a tear that fell for no reason.
For naturally I didn't say all that, she's made me say so many things I didn't say. But my own thoughts are not so different (especially when I'm by myself, and tonight, I'm all by myself). My heart is heavy in my empty house, but I blow my nose and that's the end of it.
It would be good if she'd stop making me say things I've never said.

MY TURN!
SHOUTS THE MOTHER CHARLOTTE

I knew it: she is afraid.
She's always been fearful.
When she was a child, I put her into her own bedroom, then I had to move her cot back in with me.
She is afraid.
I knew it.
I knew she was fearful.
I know my own daughter.
She's no mystery to me (there's nothing about her that I don't already know).
We shared a bedroom until she was fifteen.
Because she was fearful.
—It's my turn, says the mother Charlotte, and no one shall prevent me from playing when my turn comes around.

The shepherd will come by with his little cart, to help with the move.
He's thirty years old.
At thirty, a man is strong. He can help someone move.
We'll take the mule.
Léa will be there,
(and the mule's little bells).
—Of course I'm coming, says the mother Charlotte.
—We'll be there, shout Marthe and Élise, from the doorway of the hotel.
And Maurice will lend a hand with the bigger pieces.

She has every right to take some bits of furniture back to her mother's house.
It would be absurd to leave them there, in the isolated house on the main road bordered by plane trees.
Everyone knows how furniture gets damaged in an empty house.
The dead eyes of abandoned houses on main roads bordered by plane trees.
And with what races by on such roads.
Nowadays more than ever.
The adventuring faces of victorious motorists.
What do you expect?
That's why we're walking.
Along the main Provençal road, banked on each side by the stony rubble of the parched hillsides.
The ruined tower lording over us from every direction,
turning, turning at random around the twists and turns of the dusty track.
—I'll not take every single thing, Lili says. The house belongs to my deported husband, after all. When my husband, who was deported, when my husband comes back, he should come back to his home intact.

(IN DACHAU)

—Lili, I'm thinking of you. I'm thinking and I think: Lili.
Nothing more, a word, and such a simple word, it's more than enough. Your name—so right for the wife of a deported man.
Lili, so short, so brief, peaceful, it alone stands in for the rush of thoughts, memories, hopes.
If I still have hope, it's because of:
"Lili."
The house, the garage, the dining room, the main road.

"Lili."
In the fog of a hopeless present:
"Lili."

—Naturally, says Lili, he should have a few things to come back to.
The mule and its bells lead the procession.
The dusty track pounded by the sun.
This is a house-moving party.
It's a beautiful day to walk the furniture.
—You're not the only one, says Marthe. Lots of girls are doing exactly the same, going back to live with their parents. It's all the rage. It's this season's misfortune.
Then she cries out:
—Where's Léa?
—She's coming, shouts the mother Charlotte.
—I thought she was with the shepherd, shouts Lili.
No, shouts the shepherd, she's talking with Élise.
—What are they saying?
—No idea, says Marthe turning around.
—They're going on and on about something.
Here, there, walking ahead, bringing up the rear, the characters, the slow, loaded little cart, the twisting landscape, the staring sun, the distance they've covered.
—You're falling behind, shouts Lili.
And Maurice:
—When we get there, we'll drink a pastis.
—Take it all, Lili, take it all, we'll fit all these bits and pieces very nicely in my new house. Why didn't you take everything?
On Sundays we'll be turning customers away from our sunny windows and doors, the flowing wines and uncorked bottles. So many corks popped and poured, Lili, into raised glasses.
I have taken the things I want.

We'll put everything on the ground floor, the mother Charlotte is saying, upstairs isn't finished yet. The woodwork, the tiles, no matter.

We'll get to work immediately.

We'll open for business as soon as possible.

What do you say Lili?

What do you say Lili? Fortune is on our side.

—I won double, shouts the mother Charlotte, I won double.

—I don't quite see, says Marthe, how you'll manage both businesses at once.

—We'll open Saturdays and Sundays, replies the mother Charlotte, I've been planning it for a long time. It's ready. It's ripe. It's ripened. It's cooked.

Lili will stay here two nights a week.

—I'll sleep there, says Lili.

—I thought you were too afraid to, shouts Élise, who can hear everything they're saying from a distance.

—I thought you were too afraid to, shouts Élise, and she walks into the new house carrying two chairs made from moleskin and chrome, her footsteps echoing on the freshly tiled floor.

—This is all good-quality stuff, the men are saying.

—Tomorrow we'll go back and get the bar.

Meanwhile Lili is saying to Élise:

—I've forgotten my fears. Maman helped me forget them.

When I'm working for Maman I'm no longer afraid.

I'll have enough to keep me busy, to forget my fears.

—What will you call your new establishment? asks the shepherd.

They all look at each other:

—I haven't given it a thought, says the mother Charlotte. It needs a name, what shall we call it Lili? Lili, you should have a say.

You'll be running it with me.

—You should give it a beautiful name, a woman says, something special, out of the ordinary.
—We'll call it "the New House," says the mother Charlotte, not wasting any more time on the matter. And we'll put a little sign up on the main road, to attract customers.
Then she repeats:
Lili will be running it with me.
Everyone shouts:
Let's raise a glass to the new woman-in-charge!
Maurice pours the pastis.
Some standing, others leaning, here and there, a few more seated amid upturned bits of furniture, objects in the wrong place, in the bright white room. Élise still on the threshold, perched on a chair made from moleskin and chrome, carrying the other chair in her free hand, ready to stand up and put it down somewhere farther away.
Outside, the bored mule is growing restless, it strains at the little cart, still laden with things.
The afternoon drifts and lingers all the way down the dusty tracks.

House for sale. Ivy, nettles.
Tall weeds, wild weeds.
Old screws.
Rust.
In need of a coat of paint.
Roof in disrepair.
Parched flowers.
Stagnant waters. Creaky hinges.
Loose stones in the walls.
Stricken bug remains.
You'll twist an ankle.

Trees with low-hanging branches.
No one cut them back in the spring.
There was no spring.
For the dead eyes of the faceless windows.
For the doors and their stiff locks.
For the dusty grilles on the windows and the aged plants.
Like something out of a dream.
On the main road, bright white and bordered by plane trees.

Which is why on a Sunday splashed with flowers and the sounds of the gramophone, the telephone, the Dictaphone, the electrophone, the radiophone, the devilish record player
in between bursts of ever-multiplying voices,
knocked-over vases,
water rippling over the glistening marble of the sun-dappled tables under dripping vines,
trellises linking up with the pillar of a terrace
and the bright space filled to the rafters with luminous air,
the joyous exchanges of merry diners,
it's why Lili, the Sundayed girl from Arles, is pouring sparkling wine into clinking glasses.
One song.
Two songs.
Three songs.
A love song.
A drinking song.
A love song.
A drinking song.
A love song.
Someone stands up to sing.
Someone claps their hands to accompany them.

Someone chants.
Someone taps a foot.
Others tap their feet and clap their hands.
Someone does their own thing.
Laughter. Applause. Kisses.
Someone gets an accordion out of its case, presses a few keys.
Someone would like to take a turn playing the accordion.
Someone plays the accordion.
Someone brings the banjo down from its hook on the wall and plucks at the banjo.
Some dance.
And the sun keeping time
rolling over hips,
swaying.
From shadow to shadow, from light to light, to the scattered sounds of crystal carafes,
half-spilled.
—So sorry, wasn't looking
a thousand apologies.
Muddled hours.

At the end of the night, when all the customers have left,
Élise, Marthe, and Lili sit around and about in the disordered room.
—It's hot, the women say.
—No, no, water for me please, no wine.
—Let's open the window.
—Let's get some air in here.
—What a success, says Élise, where is mother Charlotte?
She's rinsing glasses (Élise).
—What a success, you've made a fortune in such a short time.

The people who used to stop on the main road bordered by plane trees, they all come here now.
—Or to my place, Marthe cuts in, happy and satisfied.
Did you notice that big guy who works on the railroads?
—No, say the women.
—That big guy, shouts Marthe. I was born to have him!
—What will you do, asks Élise, when your husband comes back and you have to return all the furniture and fittings?
—No one will be taking these things back, replies Lili.
—But...
—There are no buts. Maman is very intelligent, she's thought of everything. There'll be nothing he can say. I have a very intelligent mother, shouts Lili, didn't you know?
Far cleverer than me.
That's why I always do as she says.
She's far more intelligent than I am, Maman.
I wouldn't know how to run a business the way she does.
She has ideas.
Why wouldn't I do as she says, since she's so much more intelligent than I am?
In just three months she's made us a fortune.
You who would like to, who daydream about making a fortune, you hope but you never do it because you're too stupid. Clever people can make their fortunes anywhere. It's no surprise that I'm so good at obeying Maman. It's how it should be: the idiots taking orders from the intelligent.
And I admire Maman so much! shouts Lili.
—Naturally, says Marthe, naturally, even with my hotel setup, I've never had her success.
—And she's such a hard worker! cries Lili. She has good ideas and she's brave. She has all the qualities.

The proof? She's hard at work right now, in the pantry, with the sourness of a widowed old maid minding three young children.
—Naturally, the women say, naturally, we can't all have a mother like yours. Now, let's get to work, instead of lounging around in here, in the soft blueness of the night with its thousands of hands, all trembling with temptation.
—And this return you're talking about, shouts Lili, it may never happen. Why keep talking about problems before they happen? What a mistake. What craziness. As if each new day weren't enough to heavy the heart. That's women for you.
—The wine is making you look on the bright side, says Marthe, you're a happy drunk.
Lili lowers the needle on the record player.
—Tonight, I'm happy, she says, it's true, I'm a bit tipsy.
And, looking out at the large bay tree, her face turned toward the night's inviting hands, she inhales the voluptuous perfume of summer sleeps.

Gray woolen dresses, holed, torn, pulled apart, in tatters.
Striped twills, ripped, patched, stitched back together again.
—How very unfortunate, says an old woman, to get to our age and be dressed like this.
She steps on a scrap of silk and almost slips.
—Mind, she says to Monsieur Luche, through the holes in that old thing you're wearing, we can see the runs in your socks.
—It's younger than you, says Monsieur Luche.
—Have yourself a good bout of whooping cough and then we'll see which of the two of us, says the grandmother, and her gaze lowers suddenly, swiveling in the direction of the (neighboring) cemetery as if she'd just spied a lover whom she partly desired, partly spurned.
—We'll see which of the two of us, she says.

—Don't complain, says Monsieur Luche, if the hem of your evening gown (your gown for the evening of life) droops lamentably.
—It's wartime. And in wartime, the evenings, the nights, you know as well as I do that not everything goes to plan, you old ostrich. Mother Charlotte is looking after us, what more do you want?
—At what price?! cries the old woman.
And all that we provide in silver and good humor.
The other elderly people all around, busy with their embroidery, with their collections, with watching, with dozing, with chattering, with murmuring, with darning, with nose-blowing, with weeping, with humming, with whistling.
—It's true, they say.
—We all know why Monsieur Luche is so keen to defend the mother Charlotte, says the grandmother. Don't we.
—Be that as it may, mutters an old woman, if your beloved is making money, you can be sure it's not from friendship.
Whoever laughs last laughs loudest.
Whoever lives longest shall see,
and timid glances turn furtively toward their secret neighbors in the shadow of a high wall and the dark cypress trees.
The straw that breaks the camel's back, Monsieur Luche.
Don't bite off more than you can chew.
—The new house was built with our poor money, and if it were only the money.
Everything we've given.
—As soon as I can, I'll leave, says the old lady embroidering, I have somewhere I can go.
Heads grouped together.
Torn silk dresses.
Thick twills, unstriped.
And fresh faces crosshatched with wrinkles by the passing years.

*

—Shut the shutters, my girl, and the sun slanting across the faded couch of our intimacy.
—Happy?
Happy.
The golden sun on Lili's face, on the face of the mother Charlotte.
—Kiss me.
The mother says to the daughter.
The daughter bends over the mother and kisses her.
The mother returns her kiss.
—My girl, she says, tenderly. Happy?
—Happy.
Timid smile, touching smile of a love discovering itself and a happiness declaring itself.
Deep sigh of the sun expanding within the body.
Arms held aloft before the great joyous day, at last arrived.
Not a cloud in the sky.
If we've had troubles in our lives, we've forgotten them.
If there was a past, we've erased it.
The life we have left to live is not divided by time.
But only this immense, unprecedented day of our settled happiness.
Happy?
Happy.
Mother and daughter falling asleep in the invasive heat, napping behind blinds and shutters there to filter it.
The calm, the silence of the shadowy afternoon at rest.
One on the couch, in a shaft of sunlight.
The other in the bergère chair, its doily of crocheted lace.
                              Felicity.

PART THREE

Several things happened at once.
(they always do.)
He's back.
Head shaved, in stripes, arms dangling by his sides, his skin pale from dropsy.
He's back.
Arms dangling because naturally he has nothing to carry.
His only load, his heaviest load, was the color of his eyes.
He returned.
Because wars start but they also finish.
In war as in everything else, the verb "to finish" exists, just as the verb "to start" exists.
We don't lament their start because if they've started:
it means they'll end.
Like other wars, this war is over and now:
                      he's back.
with his empty gaze and memories written all over his body, like a postcard.
There's no point asking him what he saw.
He no longer knows.
And if he saw something, he'll not tell you (it was enough, surely, for him to have seen it).
He's back.
And that's that.

Went away. Returned.
To Lili.
My home.
With Lili.
On the road bordered by plane trees.
He's coming home.
How will she like the new color of my eyes?
My wife and my house.
My work and my country.
My family and my friends.

Lili ran into the shepherd.
At Élise's place.
And they saw each other.
It isn't the first time their paths have crossed.
We've run into each other countless times before.
But we have never seen each other.
Now here we are, and because we're alone in the same room, we can't stop gazing into each other's eyes.
Gazes knitting together.
Our paths would cross all the time.
But today the air between us is being ripped apart
and bright red love is spreading like blood pooling from a wound that it's impossible to close, impossible to close, and that no one could ever repair (like a nightmare).
A hemorrhage that cannot be, cannot be staunched, it cannot be.
No one could.
Lili lifts her hand to her throat.
They both look away.
Life is a dream.

Everything changes.
Élise comes in to find them standing face-to-face, their eyes cast down: she steps forward into the red.

—An inheritance?
—An inheritance.
An aunt with a will.
They always profit the same people.
People who don't need it.
People who already have everything they need.
But to us?
Never!
No fear!
I don't have an aunt living in America.
Who is this aunt?
You've never mentioned her before.
An inheritance!
It'll ruin you.
After all the charges have been paid, there'll be hardly anything left.
—She's right, says Marthe, when Ginou received his inheritance there was no money left over, I still owe five thousand francs.
Me and luck, Marthe croons, that's how it goes.
You never mentioned an aunt.
Lili shrugs her shoulders.
—It's the same aunt, Lili shouts, who I went to visit when I wanted to run away with the young man from Transports.
—But when did you ever see her, shouts Élise.
What did you inherit?
—A flock of sheep.
The women burst out laughing.

—What are you going to do with a flock of sheep?
Is it a big flock? the women ask.
—To tell the truth, it's only half a flock, Lili explains, the other half went to a cousin twice removed. But Maman went to consult with a lawyer in Alès to make a case.
—And the cousin? (the women together)
—She doesn't need a flock of sheep, replies Lili, she lives a fancy life in Marseille.
—But if it's hers, says Marthe.
—Anyway, says Lili, to cut Marthe short, Maman wants the whole flock.
She doesn't want half the sheep. She wants double the sheep. Many many sheep.
—So many calculations, murmurs Élise, your mother's so good at sums.
—Not only that, Lili adds, she has to pay for the lawyer, and that's another sum again.
—But if you're sure you'll win, says Marthe, and it's fine thing, it makes you sound rich—owning a large flock of sheep.
But how will you feed them? Livestock need be looked after.
You have to get to know them. Being a shepherd is a proper job.
A whole flock of sheep can suddenly get sick and die. Be decimated. She repeats: de-ci-ma-ted. That's the word.
—Don't you worry, says Lili, it will all work out. And she gives a small smile.
Her eyes rise over the women.
There's a shepherd in Lili's eyes. But the women don't see the shepherd. They're thinking:
—Something's up. There's something she's not telling us. What has she done?
—If your mother had all that money, Marthe says sharply, then surely she'd get the new house finished.

—The builders have stopped working, Lili sighs.
—Why? ask the women.
—I don't know, says Lili, evasively.
Then all three go to stand in the doorway of the hotel, drawn by the commotion of the bus to Avignon, which is about to depart.
A lot of people are taking the bus to Avignon today.
—It's the oldies, cries Lili, it's the oldies!
The elderly boarders.
—The oldies, say the women, where are they going?
The elderly boarders clambering onto the bus and waving farewell, helping each other on, leaving the driver to deal with the crutches.
—Pick up my cane, would you please?
—We're off! call the oldies. Cupping their hands around their mouths.
—It's just a few old people leaving, says Lili.
Like a sudden breeze, an unsettled feeling worries the air.
—We're off to buy some thread, says an old lady.
She comes over to shake Lili's hand.
—You're going to miss the bus, shouts Monsieur Luche.
—It'll wait for me, the old woman mumbles, croons.
My poor fur coat, she says, I haven't worn it in years, I think it's looking a bit shabby.
—Indeed, Marthe, not just an impression, the truth.
Granny could do with a new fur coat.
    Goodbye forever.
       Adieu.
          Bon voyage.
The old lady trots back over to the bus.
—I hope they find some thread, says Lili, look how they've patched up their old clothes.
Because they're all shortsighted or farsighted they've darned them with great loose stitches.

An old woman, already seated on the bus, threads a needle at arm's length and restitches a torn part of her dress that a monsieur had just stepped on.
Their clothes are holding, says the driver,
but only by a thread, time to get going.
Two or three old folk stay seated on the bench in the square, their luggage at their feet.
—Someone's coming to pick us up by car, they say, turning their faces away.

Only two remain.
One old lady knitting at an iron table in the garden.
The other watering the carnations, planted in a wooden crate.
—We've already served ourselves, they say, no thank you, we've finished our light meal.
The house is so quiet, says Lili's husband.
Ill-judged remark.
The last thing he should have said.
—If you don't like the house, shouts the mother Charlotte, you can leave.
Her point being:
He came back.
He had to come back, didn't he.
So many didn't. So many remained there. So many were never seen again,
and whose last image, in the depths of memory, is fading.
But he—
he had to come back.
Everything was going so well.
We were happy.
The businesses were flourishing.
Perfect harmony.
The stilled sun.
It couldn't last, and now he's back.
Now, everything is going wrong.
I had no choice but to have him here.
I'm family.
It never rains but it pours.
Everything is out of order.
Because of a man,

who is determined to live,
who refused to die,
even when given so many opportunities to do so.
—I have to set a place for him, I have to pay for his food.
The boarders have left.
The builders are demanding to be paid.
—It's all going wrong! shouts the mother Charlotte.
That roast beef you ate at my table yesterday cost me six hundred francs, she says.
—That's fine, the man says, bowing his shaved head where the hair is regrowing gray.
That's fine, he says, rummaging in his wallet, here's the six hundred francs.
There, I'm paying my way.
I'll do anything, I'm so happy to be back.
—Dinner is on the table, sings Lili.
The meal is simple. The celebratory feasts forgotten.
—When I sit at the table, says Lili's husband, it's to eat, not to have a party.
Chewing on a large bite of bread and cheese, he stands up and with his free hand rummages in a bag left on a chair.
Not to mention the fact that my daughter is unhappy, shouts the mother Charlotte.
She shouldn't stay there with him.
It's no life—living with a man back from the camps.
He's not well!
He cries out at night.
My daughter is afraid. She's fearful.
She'll get ill too.
In a case like theirs, they're sure to grant a separation.
The man has finished rummaging through the bag on the chair.
He empties out the contents of two small pouches onto the table.

The freed jewels scatter and glitter: their stones, their pearls, their golds, their platings, their diamonds—having been accustomed to the dark for so many years they are now all the more brilliant, the more alive, richer, more sumptuous, skittering across a white tablecloth over an old rustic table (and through the open window, the charming outdoor scenes, the clement seasonal weather), on the day their fortunes were made.

All three lean over the table, speechless.

The mother Charlotte tries on the rings, the earrings, the pendants, the delicate chains, a cascade of fireworks.

They move. Reflected in the mirror, the redoubled treasure doubles and doubles again.

They unclip corsages. They pull up their sleeves. They laugh.

They dance with their heavy hands. Their weighted fingers.

They choose.

They select.

They decide.

They try on.

They desire.

They envy.

At long last someone says, under their breath.

—Who does all this belong to?

—The last owner is in Brazil, says Lili's husband.

They look at each other.

Which means?

—Which means? say the women.

Well, since they didn't come back, says Lili's husband.

I came back but they—didn't.

Some get to return and some don't.

That's how it is, so we'll wear the jewelry belonging to those who didn't.

Lili exclaims:

—What do you want me to do with all these jewels?
I've never worn jewelry before.
I'm not used to wearing it.
I'll damage them if I wear them while I'm working.
I'll lose them.
You need beautiful dresses to wear jewelry with.
We'll sell them, says Lili. I'm not the type to wear jewelry. I have a little ring that I found in a grab bag, but I never worry about damaging that.
With the money, we'll buy:
>A fur coat.
>A carpet.
>A sofa.
>A car.
>A bathroom.
>A fridge.
>A washing machine.
>Armchairs.
>Bedsheets (we need some new ones).
>A tea set (in old silver, it's so pretty).
>A slow cooker.
>A kettle.
>A toaster.
>An electric blanket.
>Hot running water.
>A side lamp.
>A dish for serving hors-d'oeuvre (I've always wanted a dish for serving hors-d'oeuvre).
>Twelve knife holders.
>A serving cart.

Lili stops talking—her gaze lost in the landscape bathed in clear air stretching out beyond the open cross window.

—Where shall we go to sell them?
Avignon? Nîmes? Marseille?
I vote Marseille.
Meanwhile, on the tip of her finger, the mother Charlotte is balancing a large, heavy red-gold ring set with a jewel, not too big, surprisingly unsparkly—the luxury of unostentation that only the very grandest people can afford.
Then, in a flat voice, she starts to recite what she'd secretly been rehearsing while Lili was dreaming of riches.
—I sent you packages, says the mother Charlotte, balancing the old ring on her fingertip. I sent you packages.
I didn't want to leave it all to Lili. I made them up for you, while you were away, in that place.
Everything I did, all the efforts I made, to free you.
All that I posted.
It all cost money. Money.
I sent enough for a thousand.
I sent enough for ten thousand.
I sent enough for thirty thousand.
I sent enough for forty thousand.
I sent enough for fifty thousand.
          for a hundred thousand.
Didn't I Lili?
—Course you did, Lili replies, though she doesn't appear to be listening. Her gaze is caught by a crystalline breeze, rustling the trees in the garden.
And for a moment her husband looks out, too, at the light hanging from the leaves.
Till the tears in his eyes blur the scene.
Tears that won't fall.
Tears that well up and are immediately pushed down.
He won't cry.

Not now.
He's seen so much.
He's seen others.
So many others.
And in his voice that returns to him from a great distance, still uncertain and stilted, because of his bad accent, he says:
—Why don't you keep that ring, then, Maman. That way we're even.

And when evening comes, a bit monotone, a bit dull, a bit sad, a bit listless, an ordinary family evening, an evening of worn-out words, colorless sentences, a lifeless evening, Lili's husband calls out, disturbing the ennui of the moment:
—Time to go home now, Lili, it's getting late.
Lili's voice makes wrinkles in the taut cloth of the hanging evening: I'm not going home, I've already told you. I can't just leave Maman from one day to the next. I'll sleep here tonight ... tomorrow I'm going to the New House.
Tomorrow is my day at the New House, and the day after that.
—I can't leave Maman to do all the work, cries Lili. I can't do that to Maman.
You should understand.
—If you think he's capable of understanding, shouts the mother Charlotte.
—If we'd known you were coming back, says Lili, we'd have organized things differently.
Why won't you understand?
And the man's sorrow bursts forth:
Not in tears. Some sorrows are so great that we forget we're supposed to weep over them. Instead, we try to understand them, to make sense of them, to explain them, to analyze them, to probe them, to dissect them, and pull them apart, to know them from beginning to end, to turn them over, to flip them back, we recount

them to discover their secrets, weighing them, weighting them, considering them, rehashing them, revising them, recomposing them, reviving them, righting them.
Our sorrows.
Our immensely great sorrows.
There are no tears for them.
But once we've finished reshaping them, then—then we can cry.
Heavily, soundlessly, furtively, greedily, secretly, holding nothing back.
Abandoned, defeated, with no more talk, no explanations, no interrogations, no questions, no answers, overcome.
That's when tears will have taken over.
But right now, Lili's husband is not crying,
he's shouting.
And the two elderly ladies, shawls tightened across their shriveled breasts, are sitting in the corner of the room by the tall clock.
—Who says he's not capable of understanding?
He understands all too well.
It's easy to understand.
He understood immediately. Instantly.
When he came back, thin as a gatepost, his arms dangling by his sides, in his glorious striped suit—he understood. He might not be very clever but he understood.
Did he understand? Oh yes, he understood.
All too well.
It's not a complicated story—it's very easy to understand.
A banal story. He's not the only one. Many others, with dangling arms and deathly faces, came back to the same scenes.
Did he understand!
My wife is cheating on me, shouts the man.
My wife has cheated on me.
Not with another man.

My rival is her mother.
My wife is cheating on me, yells Lili's husband.
He paces back and forth in great strides across the room.
I've been back eight days, eight days all by myself in a one-eyed inn with chilly locks, bolted windows, its rooms left to abandon and neglect.
Other women would try to cover it up, keep up appearances, subterfuge.
But why bother, cries the man, slamming his fist into the table, why even bother.
His face pale in the shadows.
I've been cuckolded, I've been robbed.
It's a love so large it can't be hidden.
And I have nothing to say.
I can't say anything.
His voice trails away.
He shouts:
—I don't know what they get up to together!
My word, they must sleep together.
—Enough! shouts the mother Charlotte. He's mad, he's mad, he's lost his mind, he has no idea what he's saying.
We might have predicted it: that he'd come back mad, crazed.
Demand a separation.
It's not possible, Lili, for you to carry on with him.
Lili is making little choked groans, the way women cry.
—Shut up Maman, shut up Maman, she's saying.
The two ladies leave the room, slowly circumventing the big table.
—There it is! shouts Lili's husband.
You're happy now. You got there in the end. A separation.
It's what you wanted.
He curses.
Lili is still my wife.

—Get out, shouts the mother Charlotte. She points to the door, which the two old ladies, in their haste, had left ajar.
Get out. I will not be insulted in my own home.
You're in my house and I'm showing you the door.
    I REQUEST THAT YOU LEAVE

—We'll see, shouts the man, we'll see. I'll leave it for tonight, but you'll not have the last word, mother.
We'll speak of this again. Just you wait, mother.
When he reaches the door, he turns in a last hopeful effort and asks gently:
—you coming Lili?
Then with a weary heart, his head bowed, he goes out into the fallen night.
$$43 - 30 = 13$$
And it's at precisely this moment, says Lili, that the poem of my new love affair begins.
Unlucky in love.
As always.
As it should be.
I wouldn't expect to be happy.
I know I was born under an unlucky star.
I should never have been born,
sobs Lili.
No, I should never have been born.
All over the world, there are people who feel the same.
If we were to remove everyone who should never have been born, then all would be clear.
We'd know what there is to be done.
Countries wouldn't be overpopulated.
There'd be space for us.
My place in the sun.

Without playing elbows.
Open space.
No, I should never have been born, Lili sobs,
and I don't care who hears me crying.
She's pulled the sheet over her head.
Her sobs are echoing in her close, dark bedroom, in the depths of the night.
It's because he's thirty years old.
It's because I am forty-three years old.
Because 43 − 30 = 13
Because the years passed, and I failed to keep track.
And when love, yes LOVE, appears
$$I\text{ am 43 years old}$$
$$\text{and he—he's 30}$$
—Lili, you know very well that he's only thirty years old.
It's why I am acting guilty, why I don't dare show my face, because:
$$I'm\ 43$$
$$\text{and he—he's 30.}$$
Soon, wrinkles.
Gray hair.
Sagging cheeks.
Next stop, old age.
The decline that's just around the corner for me because:
$$I'm\ 43$$
$$\text{and he—he's 30}$$
I'm in the wrong. I know it. I shouldn't be 43.
The one who's wrong—it's me. Let them blame me.
Naturally, says Lili, it's just what I needed, in my life without sunshine, the black water of this rainfall.
Because:
I'm 43
and he—he's 30

Of course he'll cheat on you. He'll find someone his own age.
It's always the way.
You're not going to change how the world works.
I've no intention of changing the world, says Lili.
I've read the magazines, I'm not the only one. There are women like me everywhere.
All the 43-year-old women
                  and he's barely 30
Even so, if I act ashamed, if I walk straight past you without daring to speak, without daring to look at you of course it's because:
           I'm 43
           and you, you're only 30
—But you look so young, Lili. You don't look your age.
Truly, and I gazed deeply into my beveled mirror, seeking beauty.
I bought some very expensive creams.
I wore new dresses.
I changed my hairstyle.
I.
I did all that.
Because I'm 43
           and you're 30.
If only I were 30.
If only you were 43.
But the calculation wouldn't be the same. That subtraction just isn't done.
—When you're married, says Élise, in tones that are a little honeyed, a little pious, a little sugary, a little jealous, a little unpleasant.
She knows that I dream of marrying him. The marriage of my dreams.
She encourages me to dream of it (so I suffer a little bit more).
—I know it won't happen, you don't have to tell me, cries Lili.
Her words are well chosen. It won't.

So she buries her face in her pillow and releases her most exquisite sorrow.
She cries, she sobs, holding nothing back, at the top of her voice, like a child.
She howls.
Because a heartache, a heartache for a love that stops at
NO
is too great.
—Leave me to howl, says Lili.
Beneath the sound of her sobs, the mother Charlotte has crept into the room, she's switched on the light.
—Lili, she says, Lili, whatever's the matter?
She approaches the bed, moved by this unfettered display of sorrow.
Lili, answer me, please.
She bends over her daughter, she strokes, she kisses.
—My little Lili, says the mother Charlotte, gently.
Lili is still shaking, like a mouse caught in a trap.
The mother Charlotte is alarmed. She calls her name gently:
—Lili.
She lifts the hair from her daughter's brow.
—You mustn't cry like this Lili. You're too old for it.
And you mustn't worry about what happened earlier.
You'll never have to live with him again.
We'll make sure of that.
—No, says Lili at last, in a thin, broken voice, no, great fistfuls of tears pouring down her cheeks. She shakes her head: no.
Throat tight.
The mother Charlotte forces her to take a whiff of eau de cologne.
She's going to make herself ill.
—Thank you, says Lili, I feel a bit better now.
—Now, tell me, whatever has got you into such a state?
Lili sighs:

                    I'm 43
               and he—is 30.
—You've gone completely mad, cries the mother Charlotte, who on earth are you talking about?
—The shepherd, murmurs Lili.
—The shepherd? The shepherd, what are you thinking? What exactly is going on? exclaims the mother. As if we didn't have enough to worry about! Explain yourself.
He loves me, says Lili, and I love him
               But I'm 43 years old.
               and he—he's 30.
They've all gone mad, the mother shouts.
All of them, mad.
You're going to do me the courtesy of putting a stop to this nonsense.
The shepherd, shouts the mother Charlotte.
Then, all of a sudden, she falls silent.
She repeats, under her breath: the shepherd.
Slowly: the shepherd.
Well, she says, shrugging her shoulders, if you love each other as much as you say you do, get a divorce, and marry him.
Lili bounces up on the bed, throws both arms around her mother's neck.
—My little Maman, Lili sings, my dearest sweet little Maman.
I knew you'd understand.
Naturally, if I love him, and he loves me, I'll get a divorce, I'll marry him.
I just needed you to tell me what to do.
My little Maman, Lili croons.
She gives her mother a kiss.
—He can look after our sheep, says the mother Charlotte. A shepherd is just what we need.

Your husband wouldn't have the first idea how to look after the sheep, and he'd refuse to do it.
The age difference doesn't matter, Lili.
If you love each other.
Don't give it another second's thought.
It's not worth worrying about.
Men cheat on their wives for many reasons.
You might be thirteen years older than him—but that's not a reason.
Or, it is a reason, but only in the way that any reason is a reason.
Enough of this silliness.
Wouldn't it be better if he were fifteen years older?
You love each other, be happy, says the mother Charlotte.
Take your happiness where you can find it. And enjoy it for as long as it lasts. You haven't had much happiness in your life, I know. You were never happy with your husband, I know. But if happiness for you means the shepherd!
Don't push happiness away when it presents itself.
Thirteen years younger.
Enough of this nonsense.
It's of no consequence whatsoever.
Not even worth mentioning.
Stop making things more complicated than they are.
What will people say?
People always find something to say.
They'll say: he's thirteen years younger than her.
It's just the same as saying: he's twenty years older than her.
Or something else in the same vein.
If someone is happy, people gossip. It's how things are.
—My little Maman, says Lili.
—You'll get your happiness, says the mother Charlotte, and I'll get my shepherd.
(and my revenge.)

THE EVENING OF THE DAY
OF THE HUNT

The shepherd has been hunting in the mountains. All day long. Now he is making his way back down to the village, along the steep, winding path. Night is falling, filling masses of stone here and there with shadow. Already, the evening cool has spread over the damp vines, toward the plain.
Bearded, somber, burdened, rifle slung over his shoulder.
Lili is at her bedroom window.
Tasting the emotion of the hour. The view from her window is of the mountainous mass and the ruined tower lording over us.
She spies the violet-colored silhouette of the shepherd in the distance, slipping its way down the winding path.
The shepherd looks out across the plain, he can see the mother Charlotte's boardinghouse. At her bedroom window: Lili, in the warm, damp evening air.
They catch sight of each other. They guess at each other. They recognize each other. They call to each other, silently. They desire each other. They love each other.
But they are too far apart for their eyes to meet.
They each try to make the other out, to draw the other out, sketching an unanswered smile.
Lili, her head and her heart empty, answering only the appeal of the night, rushes out of her bedroom, runs down the stairs into the hall and pauses, a few steps away from the front door.
He tumbles down the steep path that stops at the threshold of the boardinghouse,
pushes through a gap in the hedge.
Now there is but a small distance between them, him in the darkness, her in the shadows of the house.
Connected by the magnetic force of a love unbounded by their bodies.

Visible by dint of its intensity. A grid secretly luminous in the dark. A powerful force field holding them captive, embracing them without touching them,
charging and thickening as the space between them shrinks.
It's the reason why, behind the front door, shoved open, they find themselves suddenly bonded together.
The shadows of the house, the night, the silence to swallow the declaration of their bond.

—Perfectly, cries Lili.
I LOVE HIM, perfectly.
That's how I love him.
—Fine, says Marthe, shout it from the rooftops but let me at least close the windows.
—I'm on fire, shouts Lili.
That's why I'm shouting, because I'm speaking so naturally, you wouldn't understand.
Don't look at me like that because I am in love.
It's a LOUD love.
A chiming love. A trumpeting love. A love that tambourines. That creaks. That claims. That proclaims. That hums. That seethes. That moans. That rails. That cracks the soul. That expresses itself only in sound. That has to invent whole new sounds. That has to multiply them. That has to start back up from the beginning again.
It's true love.
—Don't get so carried away, says Marthe, you're not the first person to fall in love. We remember how it feels.
If we're trying to talk sense into you, it's for your own good. He's thirteen years younger than you.
And you want to marry him.

—Naturally, cries Lili, I want to marry him, I LOVE HIM.
I love him with this kind of love. I desire him perfectly, and that's why I want to marry him.
I want to make love to him. Perfectly.
I want to take my clothes off in front of him. Perfectly.
My whole life long.
I'll undress for him my whole life long.
That's the kind of love I love him with.
Don't call me a tart. I'm no more a tart than you are.
If people didn't have this desire, THIS DESIRE, in mind when they talked about love, they wouldn't all make such a big deal out of it, would they?
Novels wouldn't get written about it.
People wouldn't live out the novels that get written about it.
Lives wouldn't get turned upside down.
We'd all be friends. In a world without desire. Just friends.
Very cordially yours.
But there is desire in the world.
That's why I'll shout about it: I'm in love and I'll let the whole world know.
I don't care. I'll stop at nothing.
—What about your mother? asks Élise.
—What about her! shouts Lili. Marthe turns to say:
—Look, here comes the shepherd now.
Lili takes a small step back, her cheeks ablaze, her brown eyes alight, fire in her bold gaze, her crooked smile, in her clumsy, half-outstretched hand,
her voice drops,
I've been waiting for you, she says.
You can go on up, says Marthe, the room is ready, you'll be more comfortable up there, for—talking.
Once they're upstairs, Marthe murmurs:

—She'll not listen, she's crazy about him. I'd be better off spitting in the wind.
—Thirteen years younger, says Élise.
—That's how it goes, Marthe replies, either they're unavailable, or they're thirteen years younger, or twenty years older, or sick, or too rich, or too poor, if it's not one thing, it's another.
—It's not a done deal yet, Élise concludes.

—I'm a woman with a lover.
I have a lover.
We ran into Lili, she was climbing the twisting path of the dazzling mountain.
The shepherd must be somewhere up thereabouts, someone says.
Brief, brutal, burning couplings on hot dry rocks at the foot of the glaring ruins.
Amid scattered clumps of stunted plants.
The sun large enough to cover the white landscape.

And those who spotted Lili muttering under their breath as they continue on their way:
The Change.
Saint Martin's summer.
The Second Spring.
Midlife crisis.
Last gasp.
It's because she doesn't have kids.

Meanwhile Lili sings out:
Now I know what pleasure is!
Yes, now I know what it is:
PLEASURE.
And how happy she is, now, to have learned: what PLEASURE is.

The following scenes took place simultaneously.
You'll have to be able to follow the one with your left eye, the other with your right.
—Still gardening, remarks Lili's husband.
—No one else here to do it, replies the mother Charlotte.
—I thought you employed a gardener?
The mother Charlotte looks up sharply, the hoe stops scraping the stony ground.
—You'd do better to mind your own business, says the mother Charlotte, and with a swift gesture she lifts the brim of her straw hat to mop her brow.
—That's exactly why I am here, says Lili's husband,
and he makes himself comfortable, ready to talk, in the short shadow of a young peach tree.
—As you know, I've finished repairing my house, I've repainted it, greased here, polished there, I've planted flowers, I've raked sand, I've lain gravel. It smells good: fresh paint, sunshine, happiness.
Not quite happiness.
A brand-new car in the garage.
I've come to pick up Lili.
—Lili! scoffs the mother Charlotte.
The man flinches.
A dry branch cracks.
Something in the mother Charlotte's tone takes him by surprise.
Pinches at his heart.
He wasn't expecting that tone.
He'd come feeling confident, sure of himself.
The car in the garage.
The shiny fresh paint.
The new furniture.

And a set of pots and pans.
All gleaming, all brand new.
For Lili.
Because I know you like such things.
You won't use them. You didn't really need them.
But you like them.
He'd come feeling confident, chewing on a blade of grass.
Munching on a blade of grass.
And going over the list again:
> the new bits of furniture
> a fridge
> a car

And the new set of pots and pans. The pots and pans are a surprise, he's not mentioned them to anyone.
—Lili! shouts Lili's husband.
She's at Léa's house—the shepherd's mother, replies the mother Charlotte.
I can't turn her over to you because she's not here.
The hoe keeps time, pecking at the baked earth.
—I'll go up there now.
—Oh no you won't, replies the mother Charlotte. Léa's not well. Lili felt she should go and look after her. Those people helped us out during the war. We're in their debt.
The hoe is no longer singing over hard little lumps of earth, handfuls of weeded quack grass, the perfume of a garden in summer.
The man is annoyed. His expression has changed.
He's silent for a while.
He's gripped by a suspicion, something vague, unexplained, a fear.
What's going on?
An anxiety.
—I'm going up there right now.
He makes a small movement as if to leave.

The hoe starts up again, its thin clear voice filling the sunlit-shadow-lit furrows between upturned stones.
Lili's husband turns back to the mother Charlotte:
—I forgot, he says, I didn't only come for Lili. How shall we go about moving the fittings and furnishings you've been storing for me over in the New House, Maman?
I need them now.
I plan to open the restaurant on Saturday, up on the main road bordered by plane trees.
The small hoe crashes to the ground: dull clank of metal against stone.
—Huh? shouts the mother Charlotte.
—Huh? What on earth are you talking about?
—My fit... my f... stammers Lili's husband. My f...
—Your f... shouts the mother Charlotte.
First of all, they're not all yours, half of them belong to Lili, so you'll have to ask her before you take her things away.
—Huh? shouts Lili's husband.
We'll see about that.
You'll see how we'll see.
Just you wait and see.
Huh?
I'll go and get them now.
My f... my f...
The mother Charlotte, gently:
—Those jewels you sold in Marseille, they were yours, were they? They were yours in exactly the same way as those fittings are mine. You knew where your friend lived. You had the address of the family in Brazil.
Lili told me.
They asked for them back but you never replied.
Huh?

The fridge.
The car.
The furniture.
The paint job.
The flowers.
    And the new set of pots and pans.
                      Huh?
—Oh that, Lili's husband groans inwardly.
His cheeks are burning. Oh that.
—And I will turn you in, says the mother Charlotte, softly.
You make trouble for me and I'll turn you in.
You make a scene and I'll denounce you.
—You can't do anything, says Lili's husband
and
you're talking like a crazy woman.
But he's afraid, and says no more about taking back all the fit…
He walks away.
If.
If she.
If ever.
What could she do?
What to expect?
Deep inside his pockets, he balls his hands into fists. Life is hard.
Life begets hate.
Hatred balls hands into fists deep inside a person's pockets.
Hatred furrows brows, chases all warm feeling, goodness, goodwill, serenity, smiles, song away.
—I hate my mother-in-law, shouts Lili's husband.
At the gate he turns back, his fist raised, and shouts:
—I'm still going to go and get Lili!
The hoe starts up its short, its brief, its dry, its sleepy, its lulling little tune again, sonorous and indifferent.

—Let him try, mutters the mother Charlotte.
Clumps of uprooted grass and mint.
Then she stands up straight, her hips aching, a worried expression on her face,
discomposed and anxious, with a shadow of surprise.
For the problem is this: the boardinghouse is not making any money. The New House no longer attracts customers who are no longer slowing down on the twisty back roads. Engines can no longer be heard stalling on the narrow track.
If.
If, faced with the future.
The future always to be reimagined,
rebuilt,
reconstructed,
redone,
redrafted,
recalculated,
reprojected, restarted, re-elaborated, redreamed.
In a low voice:
—These days I can't even afford a gardener.
One hand rubbing the base of her spine, seeking out the aching spot, she picks up the tool again.
And the clear song sings out in the silence of the waning afternoon.

Lili has tied a colorful scarf over her broad straw hat. Knotting it under her chin.
A jaunty wicker basket dangles from the crook of her left elbow.
She's a shepherdess.
—Hey hey!
Élise and Marthe hail Lili from the porch of the hotel where they stand chatting, nonchalantly.
—Hey! Where are you off to?

Lili crosses the square.
And her white wicker basket.
Her knotted scarf.
Just the women, chatting among themselves.
—She's going to tell us all about her love life.
Excitedly, they shout:
—Aren't you coming over? You've easily got time.
Where are you rushing off to?
Why are you in such a hurry?
        Her knotted scarf.
        Her wicker basket.
Come and have a chat. You've got something to tell us. We're bored.
Come and tell us all about it.
        Lili, her scarf unknotted
        her basket set down.
—Come in, sit down in the cool.
—Tell us, Lili, tell us how it's going.
You're living at Léa's; you see the shepherd the whole day long.
—Oh, Lili trembles, clasping her hands together, ecstatic, gazing up at the sky:
(she's been bursting to tell them)
He's all strength, all light, she says.
She chatters on for the women who drink up her words.
—The evening of that day he went hunting—I've never loved him as much as I did that night.
He was coming down the mountain,
I was at my bedroom window.
and softly:
        Robin Hood
The women chewing their lips, so keen to bring her back down to reality:

—It's physical, the women exclaim.
Physical! shouts Lili, that's all you can say?
I've told you what I have to say about that.
—It's just physical, the women exclaim. It won't last. You shan't make such a stupid mistake. Getting a divorce to remarry.
—Naturally, replies Lili, it would sicken them if I were happy. They'll find every reason to make me give up the shepherd.
It *is* physical, cries Lili, that's just it. And that's why I'm getting a divorce to marry him. The body comes first.
It's because I give him my body that I'm handing him my heart.
It's because I desire him that I love him tenderly.
It's because he makes me happy (Pleasure is Happiness) that I give him all my affections. It's an exchange. A kind of love for myself that I redirect onto him out of gratitude.
The caresses of the heart follow on from those of the body.
—Where did you read that? asks Marthe. You didn't come up with that all by yourself.
—You're right, says Lili, I read it, can't remember where, but I understood it because it captured my own experience so perfectly.
And all the paltry tendernesses of your moldy marriages stem from the fact that your desire was never truly desire in the first place, just a mix of aspirations that could only ever give rise to mixed feelings.
—Love is making you more intelligent, says Élise.
Indeed, says Lili, then she adds: a great love story such as ours is a rare thing, the pure attraction required to produce it is extremely rare. Which is why great passions so often spark between two people whom no one would ever think of putting together.
—You're talking rubbish, cries Marthe, and you'd be better off burning those stupid books. I have a great deal of affection for Louis but that doesn't stop me cheating on him.
—That's because you're a tart, says Lili.

—She's gone completely cuckoo, sighs Élise.
Naturally, bawls Lili, you'd prefer it if I were just his mistress, wouldn't you. Léa would too.
Because neither of you are capable of understanding what true love is. It's too much for your minds to comprehend.
—Come on, puffs Marthe, come on, there's not a woman on the planet who hasn't experienced true love. Please. Come on. Don't exaggerate.
There's nothing you can tell us that we haven't heard before.
—When I was in Nîmes last Sunday, I saw a poster with the line: "One day my prince will come." I thought of you, Lili, says Élise, in a voice that's a bit honeyed, a bit sweet, a bit cloying.
For there's no doubt in her mind that Lili will be disappointed. She can't imagine it playing out any other way (she too has experienced True Love. But that's another story, a limited-edition story reserved for a few select people, herself among them).
As for poor Lili, let's not crush her dreams immediately, for she'll be disappointed soon enough. Let's let her believe that her dreams will come true. Let's encourage her fairy tales so that when it does happen her disappointment will be even harder to swallow. For wouldn't it be good to see Lili live out her TL and at the same time get brought down a peg or two. Level with Élise.
That's what the cheap painted lips are really saying when they trumpet, in all caps: ONE DAY MY PRINCE WILL COME.
But the worst of it is that her bitter disappointment, their sinister prognosis, is approaching so fast, so swiftly, so quickly, it's so near (her misfortune): the kind of cruel, inevitable, painful, mortal disappointment that alters your looks and takes the shine from your hair.
For in their fluttering, fickle hearts women know the only outcome.
—Oh look, says Élise, my lipstick has rubbed off. And she repaints her mouth in her pocket mirror.

What's all this about Léa being happy about it? asks Marthe.
Lili goes on:
—You're all the same. You're only happy if someone else is unhappy.
That's what their friendship is like. Their friendship: so old, so real.
A bond of friendship that's so hard to break. That will never be
broken despite all the bitter words, the veiled insults, the unspoken
crude remarks.
You're all the same.
They're awaiting my downfall.
Today, at nap time, I got undressed to be more comfortable, then
I heard a loud noise in the stairwell,
startled and not thinking straight, I went out in just my slip.
The shepherd must have heard the same noise, because he came
out onto the landing too. Then Léa appeared and pushed us both
into the shepherd's bedroom. She locked us in.
—And then? the women want to know the rest.
—Nothing, Lili concludes. There are two single beds in the shepherd's bedroom. We went back to sleep. I forgot to ask where the noise came from.
—It's like a joke without a punch line, mutters Marthe.
—I'm not making it up, says Lili, it was Léa's way of giving us her permission. Telling us that we could.
—Naturally, shouts Marthe, and she leaps up, for she's had it up to here with Lili's stories, naturally, for she knows full well that Léa is not the kind of woman who'll take kindly to a daughter-in-law. The shepherd was raised knotted to her apron strings.
He adores his mother.
—As do I, murmurs Lili.
She's the one calling the shots, Marthe goes on. You're forty-three years old. She's forty-nine. She's a woman just like you. You'd better be prepared. Once you've divorced your husband, you're going to have to get her on your side. When are you getting the divorce?

—It's underway, says Lili.
Which isn't true. She's lying, outrageously. But she has to find a way to convince these women that: yes, she did the right thing, yes, she'll live her dreams, this great love story will come true, yes, the shepherd loves her, yes, he'll give up everything for her, he'll forget all about his mother.
She has to shut these women up. Prove them wrong. And put a stop to this torment, the torment of their remarks.
—With him, Lili exclaims, I'd go to the ends of the earth.
—And what about your own mother? the women ask.
—What about Maman, Lili says, calmly.
—Who'll foot the bill for the divorce? asks Élise.
—Maman, replies Lili.
—Damn her mother's got some money, mutters Marthe.
And from that point on they look at Lili a bit differently, with a touch of admiration.
So, the divorce is underway.
If she can make it happen.
So much the better.
It doesn't cross their minds that Lili might be lying, shamelessly. They're just as good at telling lies as Lili is, but when it comes to believing other people's, their hearts are as trusting as a child's.
Believing lies and doubting truths. A reversed form of clairvoyance. Liars themselves and yet so credulous and easily taken in. It's because their own lies are only ever harmless, well within the bounds of their childish day-to-day. Anything beyond that doesn't count, it isn't real. And Lili isn't really lying, she simply enjoys daydreaming about happiness, for fear of never experiencing it in real life. Like a child.
—Yes, says Lili, I will marry him. Because it's not about lust, it's love.
—Fine, say the women, best of luck, thanks for the visit.
And Lili stands up to leave, her hand over her heart, a charming smile playing across her lips, making light of her triumph:

—I don't know what's wrong with me, she says, I don't feel so well. All this adventure has been causing havoc with my health.
The heart fails.
She walks off, her hand over her heart.

> The smile charming
> The scarf reknotted
> The basket wicker

No sooner is she out of sight than her husband crosses the square in the opposite direction—for at this point all the scenes in Lili's life are overlapping, intersecting, running into one another. Hearts shattering everywhere at the same time.

Lili's husband waves to his wife's friends who've just bid a long goodbye to:

> The gentle smile
> The crisscrossed scarf
> The dangling basket

He calls out:
—I'm on my way to Léa's to bring Lili home.
The women shout in reply: one with her hands raised, the other with both hands cupped around her mouth.
—You won't find her there, they say.
She just this minute left for Blanche de Laudun. She'll be gone awhile.
We kept her talking.
—Today is full of obstacles, says Lili's husband.
What time do you think she'll be back?
—Count at least three hours, the women say.
—Fine, says Lili's husband (he's lying, he's furious).
I'll wait.
As he says this, he crosses the square to where the women are standing. I'll eat here tonight, Marthe, he says, but for now I'll have a drink. And if there's anyone around, I'd gladly play a hand of belote.

—Come in, says Marthe, come on in.
She is full of sympathy for the man.
Élise goes home.
Marthe doesn't say a word about Lili to her husband. Because she's a true friend, she won't betray her.
For Lili, says Marthe, speaking to her in her head as she prepares the evening meal, I might be trying to crush your dreams, but it's not because I don't love you.
—I love Lili dearly, says Marthe, out loud.
Lili's husband hears her say it; it makes him happy.
And Lili, says Marthe, continuing her private conversation: you must know that we don't mean the things we say, we're only playing, we don't want you to be unhappy, you mustn't think that we don't wish you well, it's just that we can't help tormenting each other.
Over her pots and pans, thoughts run out of her head and she can be overheard saying:
—I don't know why I was so mean. But I'm talking to myself now, says Marthe,
and she laughs as she turns toward the men playing cards.

KILLINGS

Words tangling.
Curses wrapping around each other.
Faces covered, half-hidden.
Two mouths in a single face.
Two shouting mouths.
Three eyes.
Half a nose.
One part blond hair.
Three-parts black crepe.
Movement, change.
A great jumble.
—Who's to know what kind of woman you are, shouts Léa.
Who's to know what kind of woman you are.
He can't be her first.
Surely she's had lovers before,
she's a girl.
Male voice. Female voices. Sobbing.
Thirteen years younger. A divorcée in the family,
(they're at Léa's, in the main room of her farmhouse).
—This isn't going to end well, mutters Marthe (in the hotel bar, in the style of a train-station buffet).
The decors mixing together.
Commotion. Rooms collapsing into each other.
My daughter's husband, shouts the mother Charlotte.
My daughter's husband.
Exterior scenes cut with each other.
—I love him, Lili sobs.

I love him.
—This isn't going to end well, hums Marthe.
—I'll kill myself, shouts Lili.
I'll kill myself.
The shepherd will, too. He told me so.
We'll kill ourselves
because:
we can't live without each other.
—I'll kill myself, shouts Lili's husband.
I'll kill myself if you don't come home with me.
And why does she refuse to come home?
And will he kill himself?
Do you think he will?
Will he do it?
Will they do it?
—I will! I'll kill myself, screams Lili in tears.
I can't live this life any longer. It's too much. It's too much.
We'll kill ourselves.
We all will.
What's the point in living? Without you.
Without him.
Without her.
—I'll kill him, cries the shepherd.
I'll kill your husband.
He wants to take you back? Let him try.
And he brings his gun down from the wall.
—My love, trembles Lili, my love,
 Please,
—Son, you're mad, exclaims Léa.
Now she's turning my son into a murderer.
The father who hasn't said a single word

                              for many many years
draws up to his full height, his head touching the ceiling, takes in
the shadows and the tormented bodies, the deranged faces.
The father stands up and, with a voice like thunder, he curses.
—That's enough! shouts the father, grabbing a melon from the table
and lobbing it at his son's head.
—Oh oh! wail the women
        he's going to kill you my love
        he's going to kill his own son
        he might have killed you my love
—That's enough, says the father, all of you, upstairs to bed.
He goes first, slamming the door to the stairway behind him.

—I'm just going to step outside, whispers Lili, I don't feel so well.
She goes outdoors, her hand over her heart.
It won't be necessary for her to kill herself.
No, there'll be no need for her to kill herself.
Death will come of its own accord.
Her heart won't withstand so much pain.
She drifts around the farmyard.
Her hesitant footsteps directing her toward the cement washbasin,
long out of use.
She has a fever. Fevers.
All the fevers all of a sudden all at once.
The fevers of sickness.
Of exhaustion.
Of love.
Of sorrow.
Of a wasted life.
a hard life, nothing gained, a life of disappointed hopes, come-to-
nothing dreams.

Her ears buzzing, her veins throbbing, her legs trembling.

She collapses in a heap on the cold ledge of the washbasin, its hardness and coolness giving her some relief.

—I'll kill myself. Yes, I will. I'll kill myself. To prove my love for you. If words are not enough, if words mean nothing now, if actions mean more than words.

If the most eloquent gesture. If actions speak louder. I choose this one: I'll kill myself.

So that words might mean something again.

It's where her husband finds her, panting, moaning, and miserable. He'd heard whimperings in the dark.

And found Lili crying, her hair and clothes in disarray.

—Lili, Lili's husband calls softly, what is it? What are you doing out here? Please, don't tell me they threw you out of the house?

—Why would you think that? Lili replies in a low voice, I wasn't feeling well, so I came out for some air, that's all.

—I've come to get you, says Lili's husband, up you go, lean on me, we're going home.

—I don't think I'm well enough, says Lili, it's too far, I won't make it. Take me to Maman's house instead. I'm not well and I'll feel better there.

He releases his hold on Lili, she remains weak, enfeebled, her body bent over double.

If you're as poorly as you say you are, he says, you won't make it back to the boardinghouse. Let's go in here, since you've said they're not angry.

THE WOMEN

—She's got nice legs, hums Marthe.

That's true, sings Élise.

It's physical, it won't last. You don't marry a woman for her legs.

—Pretty little peglets, shouts Marthe.
—Oh, laughs Lili.
Tumbling laughter.
—It'll never last, purrs Élise.
You don't say.
It was never going to happen.
Seated on the edge of the old washbasin.
That's where he found her.
The shepherd never came out to look for her.
It couldn't have lasted, says Élise, with forgiveness. (She forgives the shepherd.)
Because:
> no, Lili shan't be happy
> no, she'll never know happiness

Élise is "against."
Both women are "against."
Against Lili's big dreams of love and happiness.
Just because. For the sake of it. For no good reason. They just "are."
It's in their nature to be "against" their best friend's happiness. A happiness that risked growing greater than their own.
For without stopping to consider this absurdity, it pleases them to see her suffering.
Suffering excites them. After gossiping about Lili, they're far more active in their work. Life is more interesting when someone else is suffering. A suffering starved enough to gobble up a whole life (Lili's life).
And the little they know of her suffering feeds their sadism, secret and perverse.
—That pooooooor Lili.
—My pooooooor Lili, purrs Élise.
A bit disdainfully, a bit condescendingly, a touch superior, a touch self-satisfied and with the taste of a lover's kiss in her mouth.

*

—Ah! cries Marthe, but, then again, it's not over yet.
Then again.
Why shouldn't Lili be happy?
I do hope it ends well, don't you worry, Lili, everything will work out, cries Marthe.
—She pulled up all the carnations that were growing in the wooden crate, spits Élise.
And ripped the flower heads from their stems.
So the shepherd will see them, get it?
It's the kind of dramatic gesture you make when your heart is broken.
She read about it in *The Prostitute Princess*.
But those weren't carnations, barks Élise.
Doesn't matter, sings Marthe, the gesture is what counts.

        The headless stems.
        The trampled petals.

—After all, cries Marthe, why shouldn't she be happy?
And why is it so important to you that she not be?
—Me? shouts Élise. I never said I didn't want her to be happy, on the contrary, I love Lili dearly. We'll all go to the wedding.
—Women like you, shouts Marthe, you walk about all virtuously, clutching at your shopping bags, pursing your lips around your sharp, bitter tongues.
—Naturally, shouts Élise, naturally. Virtuous, can't say you know much about that!
—I'll take my lovers over your pinched mouths! trumpets Marthe, over your small pleasureless bodies.
—You said it, screams Élise, pleasure—that's all you ever think about, all those stories have gone to your head.
—Women like me, says Marthe quietly, know what life is about.

A different man in our different beds every night.
We dreamed of caresses, but we got the opposite. It hurt our hearts, but we're the better for it. We made love, and we're the more intelligent for it.
—And now she's saying she thinks she's intelligent, shouts Élise, that truly takes the cake.
She rushes out.
—Why, you're jealous! cries Marthe, chasing after her. You wanted the shepherd for yourself.
—You're off your rocker, replies Élise, completely off your rocker, only, Élise mutters,
only, Élise stutters, sputters.
I love Lili dearly and I don't want her to be unhappy.
—No, says Élise, her voice like butter, I wouldn't want that.
But then again, there are so many reasons to put a stop to this happiness
       that will go wrong
       that will turn out badly
       that will fade anyway
       that will end
I'll find them, yes I'll find them
               for certain
               for sure
Yes, I'll find them, utters Élise,
flutters Élise.
—It stands to reason, cries Élise, that you're unhappy with your life it was always your dream to be a kept woman.
—Like all women, my dear, fusses Marthe, would you love your Maurice quite so much if he weren't paying for your dresses, your houses, your bathrooms?
—I'll come back when you're in a better mood, shouts Élise.

Marthe watches her go, her hands on her hips, and says her under her breath:
Stuck-up little madam, thinks she's so much better than everyone else, her heart's like chewing gum.
Quarrels.
Women's quarrels. And in the hotel bar and dining room (train-station-buffet style), by the stove, the ashes are unswept.
Marthe, a tear on her cheek. She's angry.
In the doorway, the beaded wooden curtain is still making little clicking sounds, agitating after Élise.

—Drink, Lili, drink,
Lili's husband is crooning.
You can't come home in the state you're in, but I'll be counting on you tomorrow, Lili. Around ten o'clock.
Drink up.
Then he leaves, not sure whether to close the door behind him, pointing with a last gesture at the cup of linden blossom tea he's been urging her to drink.

KILLINGS (*continued*)

Scraps of day and scraps of night.
Color set off against color.
Patchworking.
If the sounds of footsteps running could be heard on the shadowy paths.
Stones rolling under the soles of espadrilles.
Branches snapping here and there.
It's because:
    Lili
       or Élise

>> or the shepherd
>> or Lili's husband

was up to something, here and there, on the shadowy paths.
If heavy male footsteps were heard
>> stepping from stone to stone

the lighter female tread
>> from grassy patch to grassy patch

the creak of parting bushes
It's because:
> the shepherd
>> or Élise
>>> or Marthe
>>> or Lili
>>> or Lili's husband

was up to something, here and there, at the upright hour, in the midday heat.
>> around about the boardinghouse.
>> here and there.

In the shade (how cool it is, at last a bit of shade) of the climbing, twisting, rolling paths all around the boardinghouse.
>> Here and there.

As the clock strikes, footsteps to the right or to the left, backward or forward.
Moving away, turning back, approaching, withdrawing.
A branch moves.
I see him.
What's he up to?
Is that her?
Watching, waiting.
Spying. Holding our breath.
Leaning. Waiting.
Wait.

It's taking so long.
What are they saying?
I can only hear the murmur of low voices.
Every now and then a word reaches me.

Lili's husband is at the boardinghouse.
The mother Charlotte told me.
The shepherd is on the hunt.
He's going to kill Lili's husband
who's come to bring his wife back from her mother's house.
Lili who had refused to go back to the inn on the main road bordered by plane trees.
Lili who'd said:
I don't feel well, I'm going to Maman's house. No one looks after me the way Maman does.
—No, Lili cried, I'm going back to Maman's.
She went home to her mother's, shouts Léa.
There's no point in you climbing all the way up to our place, you won't find her here.
Go back the other way.
—I sent Lili's husband back down to the boardinghouse, shouts Léa.
I'm on my way to the boardinghouse! shouts Lili's husband
                                        to bring Lili home.
—I saw him, Lili sobs.
I spotted the shepherd on the mountain.
He was turning around.
He's coming back down.
His mother told him.
He'll kill him.
A crime is going to be committed.
For my sake, sobs Lili

                    (the bride is so beautiful).
—Stop him, sobs Lili.
He's armed, he went off hunting. I saw the gun.
—If you can't then ask Élise, sobs Lili,
—Élise, calls Marthe, one minute, please, it's important.
(a man's life is at stake.)
The shepherd is about to do something stupid.
The shepherd is coming down the mountain, heading for the boardinghouse.
To kill Lili's husband who went to get Lili who went home to her mother,
                                        shouts Marthe.
—that's proper cinema, whistles Élise, just like at the movies.
I love it, whispers Élise. Naturally, I'll go.
I'll climb the paths and intercept the shepherd, chitters Élise.
If there's a fine role to play in this story, I'll play it, chitter chatter.
I'm not the killer.
I'm not the victim.
I'm not the cuckold.
I'm not the suffering wife.
I'm not the jealous lover.
Which is why, with a light step, her cord soles bounding up the donkey tracks, Élise goes off in search of the shepherd who wants to kill Lili's husband who went to the boardinghouse to get Lili who went home to her mother's (her plan is to talk him out of it).
Which is why, at the very same moment, on the steep paths all around: the sounds of espadrilled feet leaping from stone to stone, keeping time with their leaping bursting hearts.
—that's enough,
        shouts the mother Charlotte.
                vicious exchange of words.

Lili   home
                                                                             pots and pans
              sobs Lili's husband
making her   ill
                                                                   don't
          you
                        fresh paint   plane trees
—Leave, shouts the mother Charlotte,
will it all be over soon?
divorce
                              divorce
          yes
                    what?
—She wants a divorce, shouts the mother Charlotte.
                              Do you never understand anything?
No, he doesn't understand.
He'll be the last one to get it. He knows nothing.
Everyone else knows, apart from him.
Open   eyes
                    shouts the mother Charlotte.
—Don't you know   how to look?
                                        don't understand
          shouts Lili's husband.
And Lili sobs, her face in both hands.
—You want a divorce.
                    Why, Lili. Tell me.
Lili sobs, her face in her hands.
Why does she all of a sudden want a divorce?
Who gets divorced for the sake of their mother?
No, shouts the man, NO.
We'll soon see who's in charge.

I don't want to lose you, Lili.
You're my wife.
I love you.
It takes two people to get married.
It takes two people to get divorced.
I'm your husband, Lili.
You're mine.
Lili sobs, her face in her hands.
Why, Lili, will you tell me that?
You can't do this to me?
> Lili,
> begs Lili's husband.
You're my one true love.
You're the great love of my life.
Did you not know?
—Now he's talking about true love, sobs Lili, her face in both her hands.
I'll kill myself, cries Lili's husband.
If you leave me, when I get back to the inn, the house will be silent, lifeless, it'll reek of death. I have no one to talk to there.
—He's going to kill himself, sobs Lili, her face in both her hands.
—But why, Lili?
He still can't understand.
The idea hasn't even occurred to him.
There's only ever one reason, shouts the mother Charlotte.
He ignores her as he calls out:
—Lili, I'll give you until this evening. Think it over, Lili.
—She's already thought it over, shouts the mother Charlotte, and that's enough now, leave, this whole scene has gone on long enough.
She has her reasons for wanting a divorce.
It's because you make her unhappy.

It's because.
In the bushes, the shepherd makes a rustling sound. He's shifting position.
—They truly believed I was planning to kill a man, says the shepherd, what a joke. I wanted to pretend. That's all.
They thought me capable of committing murder, but I'm only good for eavesdropping.
They truly believed I was about to kill that man, that poor man.
Threatening it, that's one thing. Love inspired me to threaten him, what more do you want?
—Leave, shouts the mother Charlotte.
And that's why everyone left.
The same way they came.
Scrambling soundlessly down the steep, stony tracks.
Pushing foliage back into place.
Straightening branches.
And loose stones rolling ahead of them down the mountain, displaced by their scurrying steps.
It's why everyone went home.
Marthe (who, after some deliberation, had also decided to come along)
   Élise,
      The shepherd,
          Lili's husband.
Nothing happened.
No one died.
And Lili sobbing, her face in both her hands, as her mother paces up and down, silent and frowning.

Their paths cross at the bottom of the mountain.
Élise's and the shepherd's.
—First she'll have to get a divorce, cries the shepherd,

and then we'll get married.

That house you can see up there in the distance is mine and that's where we'll live

Good, good, breathes Élise, now calm down and go home.

That's your mother approaching on the main road. Tell me if I'm seeing straight. She's out of her mind with worry.

Marthe's and Lili's husbands.

—She wants a divorce, cries Lili's husband, but why?

No reason. She has no cause. It's her mother.

She's bewitched by her mother.

      But wh?

         But wh?

cries Lili's husband.

Then all of a sudden, at the foot of the slope, he comes to a halt. He turns to look up at Marthe, who is coming down the path behind him.

      Wh?

         cries Lili's husband.

The truth dawns on him.

The mother Charlotte's words had slowly done their work.

There's only ever one reason, she'd yelped.

Then Lili's husband shouts:

   Who?

      Marthe, who? I want to know

         who?

How should I know, puffs Marthe, and stop squealing like that, you sound like a piglet at the slaughter.

—Why didn't you tell me? shouts Lili's husband.

—It's not a thing people say, puffs Marthe,

and

please, stop shouting, I'm not deaf.

The truth glimmers again, he murmurs, stammering:

The sh.   The shepherd.
                          The shepherd.
                          The sh.
Marthe says nothing.
Lili's husband bows his head.
They'll separate.
—So that's what's been going on, he says (he's no longer shouting), that's why she's been staying at Léa's
Since when? demands Lili's husband
                          since when?
Marthe says nothing, she's staring at the ground, at her dusty espadrilles.
—Why didn't you tell me?
—You know why, it's not the kind of thing people just say, mutters Marthe,
She turns away to see if she can spot the village rising in the other direction.
Then she sees Élise, who seems to be waiting for her on the bank.
—Adieu, says Marthe, Élise is waiting for me.
She rushes off to join Élise. She's keen to get away from this unhappy man. Let's leave him to his defeat—too true, too real, too shameful, too hard to bear. The kind of defeat that nothing can repair, nothing can soften.
Let's cut this disagreeable moment short.
—Adieu, sings Marthe.
Here she is, already by Élise's side. Lili's husband stands very still, watching them bend their heads together, swap their thoughts.
Their heads part, they link arms, then walk briskly away.
Their overlapping shadows fading into the distance.

She asked for a divorce.
She is now back home at her mother's.

She hasn't given up on the shepherd
I love him.

He couldn't stay on by himself at the inn on the road bordered by plane trees.
He packed his bags.
He left, turned back to lock the door.
With a drawing pin, he put up a sign saying
> "House for sale."

He set off down the main road in the direction of Bagnols.
He might have taken the bus but, no, he set off alone down the road, his bags on his back.
The lonely house among the plane trees.
Looking spruce.
Rustling with a bright wind
with blossoming flowers
with climbing leaves
with shuttered windows.
The house of fifty smiles
> Of one hundred and fifty smiles
> Of two hundred and fifty smiles.

Happiness for rent.
Unwanted.
A detached house, a green lawn.
> "for sale"

He left with hands stuffed into his pockets, his fists clenched with hatred.
For:
> he's the type of person who keeps his head down
>> keeps his mouth shut
>> sets off alone

his pockets bulging with fist.
They've broken my heart.
They've broken my life.
And I wouldn't break anyone's heart.
I would never break anyone's life.
For I've not had the chance.
The opportunity has never presented itself
(it's not that I wouldn't want to, it's that I've not been given the opportunity).
Which is why he's walking to Bagnols.
To work through his rage.
The kind of rage that gnashes teeth,
that bulges pockets.
—What if I were to take my revenge, shouts Lili's husband.
The words hang in the air, for he hasn't got it in him to avenge himself.
The wrong he's been done cannot be avenged.
He hasn't got it in him to unclench his fists, clenched so tightly.
He's the type to give in,
who has no choice but to give in.
Hatred held prisoner in his clenched fists.
—But if I were to take my revenge, says Lili's husband,
I'd take it sideways
                askew
                slow
and:
        yes, I will avenge myself
        no, this is not how things will play out
        they don't know me
        they picked the wrong guy
They'll learn.
They'll find out who they're dealing with.

Naturally, I'LL GET MY REVENGE.
I'll refuse the divorce. The divorce may be granted, but in four years' time.
And 43 + 4 = 47
An old woman.
A finished woman.
No more monthlies for her.
Past it.
All shrivelled up inside.
Old
her face aged
paled
crumpled
squashed.
FINISHED
47 = 50.
She'll be in her fifties.
I can break a heart.
I can break a life.
Lili's life.
Lili's heart.
It's the mother Charlotte who did me wrong.
But Lili will suffer for it.
For:
      everything plays out wonkily: love affairs, suffering, vengeance.
Life is drunk.
So go ahead and laugh, Pagliacci, you shall have your revenge.
He chuckles a little as he walks.
Go ahead and laugh Pagliacci.
(he may be a foreigner and of humble means but he knows his music; he went regularly to the opera for many years.)

The landscape scrolls backward on either side.
And his voice echoes along the empty road.
—It was the mother Charlotte, he says.

> BAGNOLS
> 2 KM

PART FOUR

The novel is taking its leave
      gently
like a fire going out
   like a fire going out
      like a fire going out.
Like a meandering stream losing its way.
Like a trickle of water parting.
Like a wind abating.
Like a sun dying.
With only a few silvery flashes left to come,
   a few tiny sparks remaining, a few little flames flickering
back into life,
     at the heart of an extinguished fire, in the ashes
of the past.
If there were tenants in the New House, they barely noticed.
(On the ground floor, the next was never finished.)
You can always find someone who needs somewhere to live.
The rent will pay the builders.
—I've no money left, murmurs the mother Charlotte.
Money runs through my fingers like a dying fire.
Like a fire losing its way.
Like an evening ending.
If there were a few clinking coins or new coins or shiny coins left over
we barely noticed,

when we rented out the spare rooms of the boardinghouse
                                                                           in order to live.
For you have to survive.
The novel is over but we—we're not dead.
If voices have fallen silent,
if cries have been strangled,
if hearts have grown drowsy,
if words no longer burst forth,
if everything has returned to order
like a flooded river sinking back and regaining its banks,
we barely noticed.
If the days are lit indifferently, with the dull glow of regular lives,
we barely noticed.
—I'm tired, murmurs the mother Charlotte,
how about you Lili?
—I'm alright, Maman, sings Lili, tunelessly.
If our flock has been reduced by half, decimated by a disease that
we could never have foreseen, we'd never even heard of it,
the neighbors barely noticed.
—Better go and get the shepherd, murmurs the mother Charlotte.
—Yes Maman, whispers Lili,
If there were a few sudden bursts of life, one or two unhoped for
flames, they were short-lived.
As you know, shouts the mother Charlotte, as you very well know,
Lili. I have run out of money.
As you well know, Lili, I had to find tenants so that we could get by.
Lili, you are well aware of all the money I lost because of that diseased flock.
You know very well that I don't have the money to pay for your divorce.
And even if I did have a few coins left over, I wouldn't spend them on a divorce.

Lili's desperate sobs.
Are you not happy here with me, cries the mother Charlotte,
Do you want to leave me
                          again?
Have you not had enough of
                          marriage?
Once wasn't enough?
You want to do it all over again?
Daughters are crazy.
At your age?
Do you have no shame?
Thirteen years your junior!
When will you be more sensible.
You'll always need your mother.
You're just a child.
Are we not happy?
We have everything. We're not as rich as we once were but we have everything.
You always want what you don't have.
I've got far better things to spend my money on than a divorce.
Lili's desperate sobs.
The tenants, overhearing, exchange glances
out of the corners of their eyes.
And mutter a few incomprehensible words out of their wired jaws.
You can hear everything through the thin walls of this house that was never built to be rented out as lodgings.
Lili's desperate sobs echo through the walls, through the plasterwork.

Then quiet days that no one notices go by.
And if there were some reflickering of a flame in a backwind, it was unexpected.

—Yes, cries the shepherd, a little bird told me that I wasn't your first lover.
If that's how it is, Lili.
If that's the way it is.
If that's the kind of woman you are, Lili.
Then there's no question of us getting married, naturally.
I'll not marry a bit of nothing.
A woman who.
A woman that.
—Oh, Lili sobs, her voice hoarse, revulsion and indignation to amplify the wailing of her sobs.
Oh, Lili sobs.
How could you?
Don't you know?
You must know.
Oh.
—And I can't come by tonight, cries the shepherd
I promised I'd.
And I can't come by tomorrow.
I promised to.
And I don't know if I'll come by next week.
To be honest I think that.
Perhaps it'd be better if.
Not for certain.
Unless.
Don't wait for me.
—Oh! moans Lili, Oh!
She's moaning because she's dying.
If anyone is defeated in this story: it's Lili.
The shepherd looks at Lili,
all those gray hairs, cries the shepherd
those wrinkles

those flabby cheeks
those papery eyelids.
I must have been mad, cries the shepherd.
How could I have?
How was it possible?
Then, with the last vestiges of tender feeling, with the last vestiges of a past tenderness, prompted by the vague memory of some joy, a softness crept into his voice, just enough to give false hope to a person still willing to believe anything:
—Go home, Lili,
says the shepherd gently,
like a last flickering flame suddenly dying back.

When other fires ignited, they weren't for us.
And the rumors of rising waters were of no consequence to us.
But not far away, in the neighboring valley, or for other people, those were the moments when their lives went to pieces.
—We all get a turn, eventually, murmurs the mother Charlotte.
Trouble doesn't always befall the same people.
The novel has shifted elsewhere, like a storm roving around, and if there are more stories to tell, they won't be ours.
Other people's stories.
It's better to be spectating.
It's the reason why they've climbed the slopes of the mountain, up to the ruined tower.
To spectate.
To look out over the great drowning, devastating, destructive spread of a blinding sadness.
—All the same, murmurs the mother Charlotte, there's a chance the waters could still reach us.

And if they reached us.

Which is why, into the silence of their everyday lives, came the racket, the din, chitchat, the commotion of furniture being moved up to the attic.

Two women and their things that are too heavy and their things that are too big for the stairwell. The weight one of them let slip. The misjudged angle.

—Idiot, shouts the mother Charlotte, can't you see that you have to lift your end up a bit farther.

Good for nothing.

—I can't do this anymore, murmurs Lili.

—You don't want us to leave it till the floods come.

—Wedge it to the right, there you go.

And the tenants in their rented rooms listening out of the corners of their eyes, smiling toothy smiles.

They lived up there like paupers. It was the low day of their lives. Its calm stifling all conversation.

Until one mealtime when the mother Charlotte cries out:

—You know very well that I don't eat bread anymore!

So you want more trouble, do you. As if you haven't caused me enough trouble.

The whole of your life.

All you've done to me.

Either that or you want to be rid of me.

Admit it.

You've had enough of me,

you always wanted to leave me,

and now that you're getting older you think it'd be simpler to be rid of me.

Don't turn away.

I know what you're thinking.

I've always known everything there is to know about you. You know very well that I have. And this is how you repay me.
To be looked after, it's not so bad is it.
I've always looked after you.
Like a princess.
You've never had to go out to work.
And now, the mother Charlotte sobs.
Now,
she continues in a broken voice.
What's the point of raising your children well.
It made her happy, that business about the bread. She'd have been happy if the waters had risen.
Don't pretend to cry.
If anyone is going to cry here it's me: I'll cry because I have a criminal for a daughter.
Pass me that bread immediately.
She full of sin.
As if it weren't enough to have chased after men her whole life.
What will become of her if I die.
What would you do without me, shouts the mother Charlotte.
What would you do?
And Lili with her face blank.
—Shut the window and draw the curtains so they can't eavesdrop on our family's shame. They listen to everything.
Lili shuts the window draws the curtains.
      Eyelids drawn over dead eyes.

The whispers of a life restored slowed to the rhythm of quiet days, healing days, days that forget, days that repair, days that have put on their sunshades to live life tranquilly, gently, buoyed by the hum of conversations hoping for nothing, leading nowhere.
—I'm going to make myself a new dress, hums Élise.
—Have you read that novel, Lili?
—I think I'm putting on weight, sighs Marthe.
—We'll go to the pictures on Saturday, won't we? The three of us?
—Deal our cards for us.
—I can't stay out too late, says Lili, Maman is getting old, I can't leave her alone for too long anymore.
—Let's have a coffee, sings Marthe.
Ah, she says, and she laughs, I forgot to tell you, speaking of the pictures, guess who I saw at the cinema in Avignon? That young man from Transports.
He was with his wife, he has a young daughter.
All three laugh and Lili shuffles the cards.

FIN

TRANSLATOR'S NOTE

Hélène Bessette often uses a *tiret*, or em dash, to indicate when a line is being spoken out loud. Usually, the value of this mark will carry until a further em dash is used to signal a switch in speaker. Often and usually, but not consistently—in *Lili pleure*, it is not always clear when a character is saying a sentence aloud and when they are voicing it internally; in other words, where public speech starts and private speech ends. In a practice so alive to the visual qualities of the page as Bessette's, it made sense to reproduce her em dashes as a way of maintaining (rather than resolving) these stretches of uncertainty. In some lines and passages, Bessette likewise chooses not to capitalize the first word of a new sentence, not to use question marks, and not to close a line with a full stop. Again, these idiosyncrasies have more often than not been repeated here rather than corrected.

Ages and the consequences of aging (especially for women) are in question throughout the novel: is Lili in her twenties or her forties? Is the shepherd eternally thirty years old? I think Bessette wants her readers to feel confused.

"Naturellement" is a word used by almost all the characters throughout the book. Since this is a novel all about interrogating what counts as "natural" and "natural behavior"—between mother and daughter, between female friends, between husband and wife, between hosts and guests, between nation-states and their citizens—it felt important to keep insisting, with Bessette, on "naturally."

With many thanks to Daniel Levin Becker, Joely Day, Julien Doussinault, Barbara Epler, Charlotte Jackson, Anna-Louise Milne, Arno Renken, Maya Solovej, the *Société des ami-e-s d'Hélène Bessette*, Jacques Testard, and Benoît Virot.

KATE BRIGGS

AFTERWORD

Right from its furious start, streams of words, like tears or rain, flood down the pages of *Lili Is Crying*. "Hell damnation, cruelty, lies, deceit, betrayal, tears, severances, assassination, calumny, perfidy, misery and death" is as perfectly representative of what's to follow in Hélène Bessette's strange—and strangely made—tale of mother/daughter/hate/love/suffocation/resentment and chronic mutual dependence, as a novel's first line can get.

Born to a divorced taxi driver and a perfumer in the French commune of Levallois-Perret in 1918, Bessette took a winding route to publication. Having first trained as a schoolteacher, she married in 1939, gave birth to two children, and spent a three-year sojourn in New Caledonia at the side of her evangelizing—and unfaithful—pastor husband. It appears that, on her return to France, now recently divorced and with custody of one child, the time had finally come for a little evangelizing of her own. Not of the God type but of the literary type, and Raymond Queneau—novelist, poet, and cofounder of the formally experimental Oulipo group—was one of Bessette's early converts. After, purportedly, uttering a laudatory "Finally, something new!" he signed her up to a ten-book deal with Gallimard—facing competition from Seuil, one of their biggest rivals—and set about trying to persuade literary France that Bessette would soon be recognized as one of its greatest twentieth-century novelists. The writer-critics Alain Bosquet and Claude Mauriac agreed, and others soon followed suit. Unmoved by the approbation of the establishment, however, Bessette stoically retained her independence and disdained all attempts to affiliate herself, or her work, with any of the popular literary movements of the day. Instead, she set about *Lili Is Crying*—with its infamously monstering subject of poisonous mother-daughter relationships—with ideas of her own. The outcome was what the author herself labeled "le roman poétique." But while Bessette's fusing of a deceptively unshowy linguistic style with high emotion certainly earns the right to call itself "poetic," *Lili Is Crying* encompasses rather more than traditional notions of the "poetic" tend to admit. Belying its relative concision, and carrying a complex web of riches within the text, it hits the page with the kind of unsentimental bravado and formal indiscipline that only early novels wrench from their authors.

The book's inciting opening sentence is uttered by Lili's cousin, the shepherd, as he drives his flock downhill to escape the mistral-fueled storm. An unsettling "Angel of Fate" type of character, the unnamed shepherd reappears throughout the narrative in a variety of guises, from observer to prophet, confidante, and, eventually, lover. Ever-present in the background, he seems oblivious to his role as harbinger of change, right up until the moment he actively refuses it. However, having crossed the threshold of his violent opening execration, the reader is promptly plunged into the petit bourgeois coziness of 1940s Provence. Here Lili's mother, Charlotte, holds court—and the reins—from within the tastefully decorated walls of her highly respectable boardinghouse.

"Lili, Lili! calls the mother Charlotte." Making sure that forty-year-old Lili, her prized possession, is safe indoors from the sudden rain. Which she is. But Lili is crying, and we'll soon know more about that. In the meantime, we learn that Charlotte, while the proprietor of her establishment, is no menial—after all, her grandfather was a "de," which means she is "naturally better" than other people. We are then introduced to our twin antiheroines via Charlotte's litany of prim observations about their inarguably lovely life—a life her good taste, business acumen, and thrift have provided. For the coddled and cossetted Lili however—"Your ribbons and your Sunday dresses;" "You always were prettier and better than the other children."—the charm of their life together falls short of that offered by the young man with whom she has fallen in love. Ignoring her mother's unyielding disdain for such frivolities—"You have plenty of time to get married. You're too young"—and repeated reminders of the utter domestic bliss in which they already dwell, she heads out into the Provençal evening and, with her friend's encouragement, spends an evening with her lover. But when the scene changes, Lili is, once again, crying. Her young man has given up everything for her and yet she finds she cannot do the same for him. "You can't break my life like this, sobs the young man. Everyone has a mother, but we don't all smash up our lives for her sake." Except that this is precisely what Lili does, and so unsuccessfully brings to a close the first of her many attempts to escape maternal dominance. In the years to come, she will have ample cause to regret her choice, not least because of the bottomless well of misandry this near abandonment creates in Charlotte, from which her relentless admonishments will forever after be drawn.

> *—Here is my daughter, returned to me, says the mother Charlotte.*
> *My lost daughter.*
> *My found daughter.*
> *My daughter who runs away with her zip-up bag.*
> *Here is my deceiving daughter.*
> *My cheating daughter.*
> *Who has no qualms about telling me silly stories and lies.*

And on it goes.

Bad girl.
Bit of nothing girl.
Bold girl.
Whore.
Streetwalker.
Girl turned out badly.
Girl gone crazy.
Over a boy.
Stupid girl.
And what of your mother?
Your mother Charlotte?

Accompanied by a chorus of Lili's gossipy, but well-meaning, small-town friends the reader then passes through the years of Lili's youth, only dropping into narrative specifics when events necessitate. For instance, Charlotte's bitter self-reproach when the unusual purchase of new underwear appears to have aided a second decampment.

No, I never buy her underwear!
Superfluous.
For once, I bought her underwear.
I should have known that something was up.

This time however, Lili's desertion is a conscious effort, made more as a bid for freedom than in hot pursuit of young love. "It's like this, cries Lili, I refuse to go off with the man I do love. Instead, I go off with the man I don't love." Ironically, on this occasion Lili finds herself pregnant. So, while Charlotte huffily bemoans the cost of hiring staff to help out at the boardinghouse in her absence, Lili undergoes an illegal abortion which she barely survives. Her lover nurses her in the aftermath and if her friends find him somewhat underwhelming—"His heavy manner has none of the lightness of a man who'd elope with a girl"—they also counsel her that a child would have been just the trick to cut the cord and reset Lili's relationship with her mother on an adult footing. But, still pinioned by her fear of Charlotte's disapprobation, Lili confesses "I didn't think of that, I forgot everything, I even forgot about the child, I didn't even think about it being a child, all I could think of was what she would say, and I was afraid." Nevertheless, and perhaps because she is now—albeit accidentally—on something of a roll, Lili forges ahead and marries her unremarkable lover. Although the newlyweds stay well away from her hometown, and the separation from her mother grows, it's not long before Lili is crying again anyway.

> —*If only I did love him, wails Lili.*
> *And she sobs.*
> *But I don't love him, naturally.*

Trapped in her enraged and betrayed isolation, the mother Charlotte also berates herself.

> *There are so many ways to love a daughter.*
> *And how well she could have loved her daughter, that mother Charlotte.*
> *There are thirty-six right ways.*
> *(But she chose the thirty-seventh.)*

In spite of this period of separation, the mother-daughter bond still fails to snap and, eventually, Lili returns with husband in tow and their shared plans to open a gas station, with a restaurant, at a newly acquired property down the road. Charlotte is delighted to see her daughter again but very much not pleased to make the acquaintance of her "Slav" husband. Not only does he speak imperfect French but he dares to do so with a strong accent. Suffice to say, his every friendly overture to Lili's mother is rejected, with ever-increasing levels of vindictiveness. Happily for Charlotte, World War II soon intervenes. Lili's husband is rounded up as an enemy alien and deported to Dachau. Despite initially insisting that she will safeguard their home and businesses for the day her husband returns, as the war progresses, Lili is slowly induced to move back into her childhood home. Then she is persuaded to abandon her husband's businesses and ultimately transfer furniture, and other assets, to her mother's new, and rival restaurant. As far as bad times go, life is sweet. Charlotte's restaurant booms and Lili no longer thinks of the husband in Dachau who is thinking of her. But as all good things must come to an end, so too the war. Charlotte's restaurant suffers from the lack of passing military trade, plus her boarders—now old and suffering the neglect she subjected them to during the restaurant's glory days—are jumping ship. And, just when she thought matters couldn't deteriorate further, Lili's husband—having had the temerity to survive until the liberation of the camps—returns and so:

> *Everything is out of order.*
> *Because of a man,*
> *who is determined to live,*
> *who refused to die,*
> *even when given so many opportunities to do so.*

So what if he finds his house empty and his businesses shut?

And when he dares suggest his wife resume life in their home, he finds himself upbraided for the cost of the packages his mother-in-law claims to have despatched to Dachau for his benefit, and then shooed away with feeble excuses by his wife. What he doesn't know is that Lili has embarked upon an affair with the ever-present shepherd. And this time, she claims, it's love.

It's a LOUD *love.*
A chiming love. A trumpeting love. A love that tambourines.

Her friends laugh with her over it but also about it behind her back. Her mother sees it as an opportunity to rid them of the faithful, hated husband and for some free shepherding for the flock Lili's lately inherited. The only spoke in the wheels is the shepherd is thirty while Lili's now hitting the heights of forty-three. So, to be or not to be? As the final third of the novel collapses around Lili's ears, the reader is left with the distinct impression that the moral of the story might be: she who cries first, cries longest.

If brief, for a novel, *Lili Is Crying* packs a rare kind of punch. Not exactly immersive, it nonetheless rapidly submerges the reader in its fast-moving current, leaving us to occasionally wonder what has just happened, exactly, or where the story has moved to in time and space. Yet, as Bessette's keen imagery soaks into the poetry of her prose, the emotional highs and lows remain intact. Adding further formal fun to the mix is the author's frequent disruption of traditional lineation, which offers the odd ladder by which one may drag oneself free of the roil. But reader, beware, Bessette doesn't concern herself with the faux logic imposed by established concepts of form and representation. For her the novel is as much an object of the eye as of the mind. This approach imbues an absence of information with similar significance to its dissemination and makes the physical whereabouts of lines on the page of equivalent importance to their correct punctuation. So even as the reader grapples through the white space in a bid for surety, amid the narrator's polyphonic monologues, all is rarely what it seems. Usually, just as we think we are climbing up, Bessette makes some disruptive intervention, such as

The novel is taking its leave
     gently

> *like a fire going out*
> *like a fire going out*
> *like a fire going out.*

to reveal that we are, in fact, climbing down. Or falling down. Either way, finding ourselves always back in the palm of the author's controlling hand.

By the time Gallimard published *Lili Is Crying*, in 1953, Bessette was thirty-five and looking to give up her day job—teaching in Roubaix, Tourcoing, and Wattrelos. Although she finally resigned in 1962 to write full-time, the road ahead proved bumpier than anticipated, given the enthusiasm surrounding her debut. All things being equal, Bessette should have found herself sprung from there into a lifetime of literary stardom. But all things were not equal and although critical success followed for a time—including multiple nominations for the Prix Goncourt—only two of her novels (*Lili Is Crying* and *Les Petites Lisbart*) ever sold more than 1,000 copies. Bessette did not receive a pension until 1971, and the intervening period was a difficult one financially, as she worked odd jobs as a waitress, cleaner, and teacher to support herself. It was only after receiving a CNL grant in 1965 that she was able to truly begin writing full time, but her situation remained precarious for the rest of her life. By the time she died, in 2000, every one of Bessette's thirteen novels was long out of print. Her passing was unmourned by the book-buying public and went unmarked even by the once admiring literati—Marguerite Duras, Nathalie Sarraute, Simone de Beauvoir, and Dominique Aury having all at one time counted themselves among her admirers. So forgotten was she that in 2006 Gallimard simply returned the rights to her heirs, with no questions asked or money changing hands. There is a baffling injustice to Bessette's complete absence of reputation and, until now, lack of English-language translation. In 1964 Marguerite Duras contributed an article to *L'Express* on the subject under the title "Read Hélène Bessette": "There are a few of us, including Raymond Queneau and Nathalie Sarraute, who admire her greatly and deeply regret the silence surrounding the publication of her novels." She offered further explanation during a later appearance on the radio arts show, *France Culture*: "A book never appears alone, it is always accompanied by other books, it is always in a given context. It may very well be that a very singular, very unusual book is thwarted by other books."

Bessette herself attributed her lack of success to difficulties of a rather less existential nature: being a middle-aged woman and mother, without an expensive education or suitably glamorous social background. The real why behind her work's failure to cultivate a readership is probably an unfortunate blend of all of the above, but with significant French scholarship on Bessette still underway, we can't know for sure. What we do know is that this innovative practitioner of the poetic novel was left behind in the dust and noise which followed the nouveau roman's success, to die in penury, isolation, and chronic mental ill-health. It is with thanks to figures such as her biographer, Julien Doussinault, who has advocated tirelessly on her behalf, that fortunately—and in the tradition of many silenced, disregarded, and dismissed writers before her—Hélène Bessette's work survives: intrepid, provocative, and untarnished, to live another day.

EIMEAR MCBRIDE